PRINCE CLAIMED

A SCI-FI ALIEN WARRIOR ROMANCE

VIVIAN STAR

 Created with Vellum

When most people win a lottery, they get money. I got a big green alien warrior who wants to claim my body.

Lucky me.

Entering The Mates Lottery, a contest set up by five alien races to find human brides to breed with, was the only way to get the money I needed to save my youngest sister.

I never expected to win.

And while I may have won the lottery,

Prince Khirrox is dead set on winning my heart...

~ ~ ~

Prince Claimed is the first of an eight-book series called The Mates Lottery. Sexy alien warriors meet feisty Earth women who steal their hearts in this series. Will they steal yours too?

Being human sucks.

I mean, seriously, we lost out when the universe was made and someone decided that humans got no powers and short lifespans, unlike the five other species that live in the universe with us. Looking around the busy market street in front of me, I can't help but notice the aliens walking around with the humans. The green-, blue-, or odd purple-skinned aliens really stand out in a crowd. This market town is a stop off place for the universe, so we see a variety of aliens. It's also one of the safest places on Earth due to the "no fighting or stealing, or you will be killed" policy. I'm sure it has some fancy name that I can't remember. Even if, by some miracle, I didn't notice the brightly-coloured aliens for their pigmentation, they stand out because humans look so small and plain next to them. They all look almost human-like but taller. Oh, and they don't wear shirts... including the strange-looking women. *Talk about awkward.*

Two tiny pieces of fabric does not cover much. That's for sure.

One gold-skinned alien—I can't recall which planet gold aliens are from—stops and pulls down his cloak. The alien's ears are slightly longer than humans, tipped like fairies or elves from fairy tales, and his skin has markings of his planet, which kinda looks like tattoos swirling down his arms. All aliens have these longer ears and tattoos.

But human tattoos don't glow.

What the aliens must have thought when they came to Earth and made their trade deals with us, the small human creatures who kinda look like them but have no powers yet still managed to nearly kill their planet, turning it into a nearly barren wasteland.

We were lucky they decided not to just take over and declare war on us in the beginning to save our planet. One thing they love, which I have learnt from the gossip magazines on my tablet, is their planets.

I guess the only thing Earth has that makes us worth trading with?

Clean, fresh water and fertile women.

"Darcie! What are you doing up there?!" Savannah, my oldest sister and general pain in my ass, shouts across the market, waving her arms around like a bird that can't fly. Rolling my eyes, I jump down from the roof of the small building, landing on a wooden crate that creaks. I climb down the seven crates before hitting the ground and brushing the dust off my distressed jeans and off-white T-shirt. It used to be white...but hey, good laundry powder is expensive as heck. I'm just lucky it doesn't smell.

"Where did he go?!" some man shouts in the distance, and I turn just as a little boy, about eight if I'm guessing right, smacks into me, and we both tumble onto the dirt. He looks at me with pure panic, clinging onto a can of processed beans like his life depended on it.

Judging by how skinny he is, it just might.

"Wait, don't run that way," I whisper, catching his arm when he climbs to his feet and tries to run. He stares at me, tears coating his eyes, and for a second I wonder if I could take him home with me and my sisters. Guilt clogs my throat when a second later, I know I just can't do that. We are barely running the farm we inherited from our parents, who died five years ago, just so we can eat enough to get by...let alone pay all the bills we have for the medicine that keeps our youngest sister alive. Clearing my throat, I point up at the crates. "Climb up those and jump three buildings over. That house is empty, and you can hide there until they give up."

"Th-an-k y-oo-u," he tells me, struggling to pronounce the words. My heart hurts for him as I let his arm go and he starts to climb the crates. Pushing my waist-length straight caramel blonde hair over my shoulder, I look down the alley and find someone watching me.

Not just someone, an alien no less.

His big frame nearly takes up the end of the alley, his body and face hidden under a thick, dark green cloak, but his arms rest at his side, the sun reflecting off his light green skin.

A strange sensation pangs deep within my stomach, almost painfully, as I stare at the man, but too soon he turns and walks away, and whatever that was, cuts out, leaving me gasping for air.

"Honestly, Darcie, what is wrong with you today?" Savannah snaps right behind me, making me jump, and I try to forget the weird feeling. "We need to get to the sign-up. It's the last day, and you're the only one out of us all that hasn't signed up."

"I was putting it off until it was absolutely clear no miracle was going to save us. Girl can hope, right?" I tease as I turn around, hooking my arm through Savannah's, and she looks at me like I'm cray cray. She sighs, resting her head on my shoulder.

"I wish we didn't have to sign up either, trust me. But it's for Alice," she reminds me, and I gulp. I would do anything for my sisters, and they would do anything for me. Alice was born with a medical condition called Exrica, which poisons her every single day, and her life expectancy isn't good without medication. Which, of course, costs a damn fortune, and even though my sisters and I work a farm twenty-four-seven, we still don't make enough to get her by anymore.

Our parents left us with a sizable fortune, but that only lasted all the way up to last year. Now we are desperate.

Which is why we are now standing outside the market building for The Mates Lottery. I stare at the huge glowing sign on the wall suggesting we go through the glass doors to enter.

"Good luck," Savannah tells me, giving me a little push to walk up the steps. Holding my head high, I only think of Alice, my sweet sister who needs me to do this, no matter the cost. The second I walk through the door, the blinding light from inside burns my eyes, and I blink a few times. When I can finally see, a human woman is right in front of me, jumping on the spot with a clipboard in hand.

"Oh, a new sign-up! I was so sure no one else would come today. Our area is not one of the busiest in America," she all but squeals.

"That's because most people are rich and not stupid around here," I answer, but she doesn't reply to me as she scribbles on her clipboard.

"Welcome to The Mates Lottery Sign Up. By signing your name to The Mates Lottery, you will be entered into a worldwide test to find suitable mates from another race. In exchange, you will be given five hundred notes, so you win either way! If you are chosen, you will be collected from your home and given to a male of one of the five races to take back to their home planet, and you will be obligated to give them a child. You, of course, will mate with them and bring up the child on their planet. Do you understand this and still willingly agree to sign up?"

Shit, she makes the whole thing sound worse than what I already knew. I tightly smile. "Yep."

"What's your name, honey?" she asks with a big grin.

"Darcie Lily Jackson," I answer, praying to all the gods I can think of that I don't get chosen. "And how quickly can we get this done?"

CHAPTER TWO

"Go after the homeless boy and take him to our ship," I instruct one of my royal guard, Strad, at my side. He nods his head and runs down the market street as I stare at the place the Earthling woman just was.

I felt it. A mating bond.

Fucking hell, I never expected that. I didn't get a good look at the female, but I liked what I did see. Blonde hair like spun gold, long legs and a hot body. I'm sure once I'm closer, I can spend my time exploring every inch of her.

"Sir, are you ready? The water trade has gone over well, and we are boarding the ship shortly to leave," Zex, my friend and the royal healer, states from my side. He follows my gaze to the empty alleyway. "Sir?"

"When does The Mates Lottery close today?" I ask Zex, who sharply turns to me with a shocked expression.

"Are you sure? I did not believe you were interested in a mate," he enquires. "Has something changed on this mission?"

"Not on the mission, no," I reply. I walk straight through the busy market town full of starving humans who are not looked after by those in charge. It doesn't take me long to get to the building where they advertise The Mates Lottery. Zex stops at my side as we both stay in the shadows and watch as two women come out of the building: the girl from earlier, my potential mate, and possibly her sister, based on how much they look alike.

"Find out everything about these two women while I go inside. No one else is to find out, especially not my brother," I tell Zex, knowing he will do as I ask and keep his findings private.

"Yes, sir," Zex replies and brings up his tablet as I walk into the building.

"Welcome to The Mates Lottery. Are you here to sign up for tonight's drawing?" a young bubbly girl asks, twirling her finger around a strand of hair. She flutters her eyes at me, running her gaze over my body. "Surely a man like yourself does not need any help finding a mate."

"I am here to enter," I coldly tell her. "My name is Prince Khirrox from the planet Strixa."

"Oh, oh," the woman splutters before going bright red and falling to her knees. I sigh, hoping she will hurry up, as my thoughts drift to the woman in the alleyway again.

The feeling in my chest was like a lightning bolt smacking me in the heart the moment I saw her.

My mind repeated the same word: mine.

Whoever you are, little Earthling woman, I'm not leaving Earth without what is mine.

CHAPTER THREE

Mashing the potatoes in a bowl, I look up as Isabelle, my second oldest sister walks into our small kitchen, covered head to toe in mud and literally smelling like shit.

"Oh my god," I mutter, holding my nose to try and save myself from the stink.

Savannah bursts into laughter next to me, leaving her job of mixing the leek soup to enjoy whatever the heck happened to Isabelle.

"That damn cow is evil! Evil!" she protests, waving her arms around. "Every day, that damn cow makes me chase her around the field, and *today* she shoved me into a puddle of mud and her poo. Urgh!"

I can't hold in the giggles as I join in laughing with Savannah. Isabelle glares at us both before trudging out of the kitchen as we continue to laugh even as she slams the door behind her.

"Animals really hate her, don't they?" I say when I've calmed down, going back to my attempt at mashed potatoes.

"Oh, they see her coming alright," Savannah agrees, with her own chuckle. Once the mash is done, I scoop it up into a bigger bowl and take it into the dining room. Our once lovely house is a little rickety now, the flower wallpaper is falling off the walls in some places, and the dining table desperately needs sanding down.

But none of it matters to us now. All we want is to live with each other. To be healthy. Money matters little when you are faced with starvation and losing your family.

Pushing back those intensely morbid thoughts, I place the mash down and head up the stairs. Turning my head, I stare at the only photo of my family we have in a worn-down silver frame at the top of the stairs. My parents stand in the middle of us all, looking proud in their beautiful clothes. Dad had his favourite brown suit on, with an antique pocket watch that now belongs to Isabelle hanging from his pocket, and his wispy blond hair is combed to the side. Next to him, though much shorter, is my mother. She had the exact same colour hair as I do, but hers was kept in a short bob, whereas I haven't cut my hair since she died. Her green eyes match mine, and dad used to tell me mum's eyes reminded him of emeralds, so bright and alluring. All my sisters and I are sitting at their feet, with me on the far left. Isabelle and Savannah sit next to me, and then Alice is in the middle. Chloe sits on the other side of Alice, and they look so different. Chloe is our adopted sister, and with her deeply tanned skin and pitch-black hair, it's kinda easy to tell. It never mattered to us, she is our family either way.

This photo was taken a year before they died, and it almost hurts to remember how happy and easy we had life back then.

We all had to grow up pretty quickly and learn how to run a farm, keep a house and care for our sick sister.

But I would do it all over again a million times because my family is so worth it. I force my eyes from the picture and run up the stairs. I knock on Alice's door two times before opening it up and heading in. Alice sits on her bed, her legs crossed and a book in her hands. Alice is never without a book, and it would be weird to see her without one.

"What are you reading today then?" I ask as she

looks up at me, her light green eyes, just like dad's, finding mine.

Tucking some of her light blonde hair behind her ear, she answers, "It's called *The Chronicles of Narnia* by C. S. Lewis. It's about a girl that finds another world in her wardrobe."

I chuckle and go to her wardrobe, pulling it open and sticking my head in. "Nope, no other world full of sexy, rich and protective men to be found. What a shame, I could use one of them."

She laughs with me as I close the wardrobe and walk to the door. "Dinner is ready in five."

"Awesome, I'm just going to finish this chapter," she tells me, her head already stuck back in the book.

"One chapter, not ten!" I remind her as I leave her room. She doesn't answer me, already lost in the new-to-her book we bought at the market for her. They basically give them away, since no one wants to read paperbacks when you can click a button on your tablet and find any book you want.

But Alice *loves* paperbacks. Something about how they smell and feel. I bang on my other sisters' rooms, shouting that it's time for dinner, before heading downstairs. Savannah just places the large bowl of leek soup on the table, and I sit down in my regular seat. Alice and Isabelle come rushing into the room a moment later, followed by Chloe, who has an old piece of tech in her hands.

"No tech at the table!" Savannah demands, and Chloe grumbles, putting it down on the side table before taking her seat.

"How was your day?" Chloe asks as I place a spoonful of soup into my bowl and a scoop of mash. I glance at my sister, whose black hair is bundled up into a messy bun, and she has a small screwdriver sticking out of the mess. Ever since I can remember, Chloe has been obsessed with any technology she could get her hands on, and I wish we had the money to send her to college. She would make a great engineer for the colonies where most of the people of Earth live. Land is expensive, and we are so lucky we inherited this place, which has been in our family for six generations, or we would be living in a colony. Those places are overrun with nasty gangs, and it's easy to die in them for doing nothing but existing. There are no real laws, and no one really owns them. It's a recipe for disaster.

"Nothing special, just signed up for the Lottery," I say, but I almost want to tell her about the strange alien man I saw for just a second. I rub my chest, right over my heart, where it hurt before and shake my head.

"Are we all going to watch the results in half an hour?" Alice asks, guilt flashing in her eyes. "I want to say thank you once again. I can't ever repay you for this."

"You never, ever have to," Isabelle says, placing her hand over Alice's on the table.

"We know you'd do the same if it was any of us," Chloe adds in. "Plus, no alien dude in his right mind would pick us. We would all jump ship before they got us home."

"They would have more luck with the alien groupies in the colony who are desperate to get chosen," Savannah agrees, climbing out of her seat and grabbing the remote control from the side. She clicks on the TV on the other side of the room, turning up the sound as I scoop soup into my mouth.

"Greetings to all citizens of Earth. Welcome to The Mates Lottery. I'm sure all of you are excited to see the ten chosen mates for this year from this district of a little over three hundred thousand people," a bubbly human woman with dyed pink hair and fake colourful marks on her skin speaks. "There were over six thousand entries, a good two thousand up from last. Isn't that marvellous?"

"Or sad if you really think about it. Everyone must be getting really desperate," Chloe mutters, and

I agree with her. No one in their right mind wants to be an alien breeder and leave their families, their homes, for a new planet.

"So, for the announcement you have all been waiting for. The ten very lucky winners are..." She dramatically stops mid-sentence as she looks down at the tablet in her hands, and I sigh. I pick up my empty bowl, standing up and heading for the door. I know I won't be picked. There is nothing to worry about. "Darcie Jackson, Olivia Charles, Julie Nuttan, Anna Patrick, Kitty Blake and, oh wait, one second."

I freeze, all my sisters' eyes fixed on me, and my hands shake around the bowl. "So sorry about that, there was a technical problem on my screen. The final names are Louisa Timms, Maisy Buttons, Chloe Jackson, Savannah Jackson and Alice Jackson."

The bowl falls from my hand, smashing into pieces at my feet, and I stare at the screen, wishing I was dreaming.

I won The Mates Lottery with my sisters.

Oh fuck no.

CHAPTER FOUR

Shoving clothes into a rucksack, I don't look behind me as I hear my door opening. They should be packing, like I told them to do when I left the dining room just a few minutes ago. We can't stay here any longer.

The frigging aliens will be coming for us.

And I'm not being anyone's breeder. No. Way. In. Hell.

"What are you doing? They won't be here until tomorrow to collect us. I thought we could spend the night talking," Savannah asks me. "You can't honestly think you can run from this?"

"I'm running," I reply, moving around my small room. I pull out a box from under my bed, pushing the lid off and taking out the pink diamond necklace that mum left me in the will. Savannah never once agreed to let me sell it when I offered, no matter how hard things have been. We each got one gift from mum and dad, and it would break my heart to sell this. The chain is long broken, making it unwearable, but I will find a way to have it fixed. I stand up and put the necklace in my bag before zipping it up. "You are all coming with me. We are not being breeders for alien warriors who can't find their own girls. That is *not* happening."

"We can't run," she softly tells me, taking the bag from my hands and pulling me into a hug. "We never planned this, but we have to accept what has happened and make our plans."

"Accept that we are going to be married off to a random alien warrior?" I reply, stepping back and pushing her arms away. "And have alien frigging babies! Do they even give birth the same way we do? Why do they have no fertile women? Why do they need us?"

"No one knows. That is a secret they keep close to home," she reminds me. "But I'm certain we will all find out soon. I'm not happy about this, and I will fight my own ground whatever happens, but I know we can't run."

"How can you be so accepting of this at all?" I demand.

"Because, just like when mum and dad died, I have to be the strong one and not the wild one like you. Or the sick one like Alice, or the empathic one like Isabelle or even the lost one like Chloe. If I break, so will my four sisters who look up to me," she says, but her voice wobbles a little.

"Sav—" I whisper.

"Alice will most likely be rejected quickly and sent home. I've told Isabelle to sell the farm, and the money will get her a safe place at a college where dad's friend works. She can then apply for aid for Alice when she comes back," she tells me. When she makes plans like that, she sounds just like mum.

"What if they just kill her?" I nervously ask, a sick feeling clogging up my throat. "Alice, I mean. It would be a big task to send her back when they realise how ill she is, and it would be easier to just let her die."

"We have to hope they don't," Savannah replies, making my heart sink and my hands shake.

"Well, I'm not hoping or guessing. I'm leaving, and you should come. So should Chloe and Alice," I say. "I will get the car, and I can drive. You just need to get in the back."

"No, Darcie. You won't get far," she urges as I pick my bag up and fling it over my shoulder. "Please don't do anything stupid and rash."

"I will not go with some alien man to his stupid planet to have who knows what babies!" I all but shout in frustration. Tears fill Savannah's eyes, and I hate myself a little for shouting at her. It's not her fault. I hug her tightly before letting go, knowing I can catch the ten o'clock bus to the colony if my old-ass car can get me fourteen miles down the road, and then make a plan there.

Alice, Chloe and Isabelle stand in the kitchen, in front of the back door, when I get there, but they aren't looking my way. The door is wide open, and in the field outside is a smooth black ship in the shape of an arrow. Upon closer examination, I see the huge ship takes up at least three fields and is heavily lit up with white lights. The spotlights shine onto the ground, and as I step in the middle of my sisters, a large metal door slides to the side before a path snaps out and clicks all the way from the door to the ground in a diagonal line.

"How did we not hear them land? The ship is nearly silent," Chloe whispers in shock.

These aliens are sneaky.

"Shit, we have to leave. I love you and just wait here. I will get the car!" I say, kissing Alice's cheek.

"Darcie, no!" Isabelle shouts after me as I rush through them all, narrowly missing their hands as they reach for me.

Without looking back, my heart hurts as I run around the house and straight towards where our old car is kept. I barely get a few feet when a sharp pain smacks into my chest, and I stumble.

Rubbing my chest, the hairs on the back of my neck stand up, and I turn around slowly. Right in front of me is an alien man in a cloak, the same man I saw before.

I don't know how I know that.

But it's true. I feel it.

"You're trespassing," I nervously point out. "*Wherever* you're from, that is illegal."

"There is someone here that is mine." His deep grumble of a voice makes me shiver—and not for the wrong reasons. "And I'm not leaving until we talk."

Calm down, girl, and think.

I need to run.

"Well, I think you are...," I start and then run, not listening to the voice in the back of my head that reminds me aliens of all races can run fast, that they are twice as strong as humans, and he will have no trouble catching me. I look back only to discover, not surprisingly, he is gone, and when I turn my head back, I smack into his chest headfirst and fly backwards in the air.

The world spins as I land in the dirt, and I hear my alien stalker mutter one single word.

"Fuck."

CHAPTER FIVE

"Her elevated stress levels are most likely the cause of her extended sleep. It has only been seven hours, I would suggest we wait longer before applying any healing remedies," a male's voice I don't recognise states as I groggily wake myself up, blinking my eyes open and staring up at...*space? Whoa, that is a lot of stars.* "She is very underweight for her age and height, which might make her incompatible with modern medicine until she is at a better weight. But she is fertile, extremely so, and with care, she will make a very suitable mate."

The man's words blur as I fixate on the view above me, just through the glass above me where outside is just nothing but stars and stars for as far as I can see. I'm not seeing them from a window on

Earth, I know that much in my heart. I can hear the buzz of an engine, that vibrating noise you get from being in a car or something much bigger. Fear clogs my throat as I close my hands and feel that I'm lying in some kind of warm water that is nicer than any bath I've ever been in. The hot water went out when I was a kid, and we had to warm our water up on the fireplace. It was never warm like it used to be.

Like this water I'm lying in now is.

"It has been too long," another male, low-sounding voice replies, and I know that voice. It all comes back to me quickly. I was at my house, and I tried to run away, but then the big alien man was there. *Heck, has he abducted me?*

Something near me makes a long beeping noise, and I turn my head just as two aliens turn around, staring me down like a tiny dot under their feet. They both have light green skin and are hella big and muscular. I don't focus on the man with silver hair, as my gaze is fixed to the man on the right with soft black locks of hair falling across his forehead. His silver eyes, like eyes I have never seen, stare right down at me as a strange feeling sits in my chest. It's not painful like every time before, but it's disconcerting, to say the least. His shoulders are huge, stretching the fabric of his top before dipping into a narrow waist. From his high cheekbones to his big eyes and soft-looking lips, he is ridiculously sexy.

"Are you well?" the shorter one of the two asks, pulling his long silver hair into a low ponytail. "We hoped you would awaken soon."

"Where the heck am I?" I demand, sitting up and shivering from the loss of the warm water on my back. The silver-haired guy offers me his hand and picks up a towel from underneath whatever I am sitting on at the same time. I take the towel and climb out by myself, eyeing my strange silver dress that clings to my body and somehow is still decent, not showing anything. I still wrap the towel around myself and back away.

Who the hell got me undressed?

"You have nowhere to escape," the black-haired dude heartlessly states, his gravelly voice making me shiver. His sentence sounds like a threat, but it might just be that he looks like a giant warrior dude, so anything he says could be taken wrong. I imagine if he said *kittens are cute*, it would sound demanding. "Running is pointless."

"Khirrox, perhaps I should treat her. She may be a slight bit confused," the silver-haired man gently suggests and takes a step towards me, but I keep my gaze on the leader in the room.

"You are a stalker, and now you have kidnapped me! I'm not letting either of you two lunatics anywhere near me!" I shout, glancing around the room. There are no doors in sight, just outlines on metal doors and touchpads next to them. This must be a medical bay of some sort; it is covered in beds filled with purple water, and medicine-filled cabinets are on each wall. It's all modern and shiny...a million miles from what I have ever seen in my life.

"You believe I am stalking you? A little human?" Khirrox drily asks. We might not be the same race, but it seems like sarcasm is a language we all share.

"If the boot fits," I sourly reply. "Now who is the smart one that can take me home before I kill you both? Which I will do if you come anywhere near me. I'm no breeder."

"No one will touch you or take you anywhere on my ship unless they want to die," Khirrox coldly states, and I feel his warning like a sledgehammer hitting a brick wall. "This is your home for now. Until we get to my planet in around eight Earth months."

I stare down my kidnapper like he has grown another head before I run around them to the large window at the back of the room. There in the distance is Earth, shining from the light of the sun, and a pang of homesickness hits me hard in the chest.

As well as pure panic.

"My name is Zex Cross, and I am the main healer on board this ship. I would like to make sure you are feeling alright if you do not mind," the silver-haired man softly asks. I turn around to see Khirrox leaning against a nearby wall, his arms crossed tightly over a plain white shirt that hugs his muscular form. A necklace with an upside-down triangle and a sparkling silver crystal of some kind hangs from his neck, and his black trousers are hanging over heavy-looking black boots.

Why can't I stop looking at him?

"Why am I here?" I ask instead, dodging away from Zex, who has some strange thin tablet thing in his hand that looks way too much like a probe for my liking.

"The Mates Lottery picked you as a mate for me," Khirrox reminds me, not a hint of warmth in his tone. "As much as you clearly are disgusted at the idea of mating with another race, we have been led to each other by fate. More than once. I believe the goddess herself is guiding our lives."

Jogging my memory, I vaguely remember hearing about some goddess of life that the other races all believe in. "I'm not an alien groupie, so you're shit out of luck. The Mates Lottery screwed you over, big guy."

His lips wobble for a moment like he might smile, and I strangely want to know what that looks like. He soon frowns once more though. "I do not believe it has. Zex, do show Darcie around the ship and to her room, as well as to the dining quarter when she is ready to eat and socialise," he says before walking away towards one of the doors.

"Wait," I demand, and he turns around. "My sisters. Where are they?"

"None of the other Lottery winners are on this ship, I'm afraid. Your sisters were taken to different planets," he tells me, and it's almost...compassionately. I hide the tears that sting my eyes, turning away, but the glass shows me my reflection. I look like a ghost, wrapped in a white towel with my wavy blonde hair falling around my shoulders. The tears in my green eyes make me look weak and frightened...and being honest, *I am scared.*

I've never been away from my sisters, and now I have to face life on an alien ship without any of them.

In the reflection of the glass, I see him turn back, continuing to the door, then pressing his hand against the touchpad. It flashes purple before a door slides open almost soundlessly, and he looks back at me once. One look hits me hard in my chest, that strange connection almost painlessly burning in my chest until he looks away and leaves.

The room seems to suddenly have oxygen once again, and I suck it in like a dying woman.

Zex waves a hand to a chair nearby, a soft expression in his eyes. "Please sit."

"Fine," I answer, knowing he isn't the enemy here. *Oh no, that's Khirrox. I now have a second person on my enemies list to go with the neighbouring farmer's daughter who cut my hair in school because it was longer than hers and she didn't like that.* I sit down, and Zex grabs a long white tablet from the side. He holds it in front of me, and it flashes purple once, somewhat hurting my eyes.

"I am sorry about that. It was a scan of sorts," Zex comments, lost in whatever he is reading. "Other than a slight concussion and the typical signs of starvation that come with most Earthlings, you are perfectly healthy," he concludes, putting the tablet back on the side and crossing his arms with a big welcoming smile on his face. "We have an excellent dining hall here. I think we should head there first. I'm rather hungry myself."

"How can I understand your language?" I ask, even though the sound of food is appealing.

"While you were sleeping, I placed a microdot in your ear, which translates everything in every modern used language known to the galaxies," he explains to me. "You cannot feel it, and it will not hurt you. I believed you would be most confused if you awoke and you could only speak to Khirrox."

"He can speak English then?" I question, standing up.

"Yes, he is fluent in many languages due to his upbringing," he answers me, walking to the other side of the room. He unlocks a cabinet and steps to the side. "There are clothes in here, and they are technologically advanced to fit you no matter what size. I will wait outside."

I nod and Zex leaves the room through the same door that Khirrox left through. I leave the towel on the chair and head to the cabinet, picking up the dark purple long-sleeved top, black trousers, and plain black underwear. Sure enough, when I slide the soft material on, it changes to fit me perfectly. Like shrinking clothes. Heck, I've never had clothes that fit me before. I wish I could show Savannah or Alice...wherever they are.

Isabelle would love this, her obsession with

clothes was always there since we were kids. Chloe would be fascinated with the technology side of the clothing for sure. A part of me knows Isabelle will be okay on Earth, she is smart and fierce enough to look after herself. But Savannah, Chloe and Alice are in the same position that I am in. I just have to hope they found themselves with a good alien dude.

Though I'm not even sure I have yet.

Blinking back the tears, I find a hairbrush and work all the knots out of my hair before brushing my teeth with a new toothbrush and paste that tastes like strawberries. When I'm done, I stare at myself in the reflection of the glass. My messy hair now falls in golden locks down to the middle of my back, and the purple shirt makes my curves look seductive rather than clumsy like I've always thought they were. The tight black trousers do wonders for my ass, if I'm being honest.

I look good.

Dammit, I do not want to be an alien snack.

If I looked bad...would the big guy send me home? I highly doubt it, he's already made it clear that he thinks fate wants us together, and it's not going to get me anywhere if I keep worrying about it. I do not care what the sexiest alien man I've ever seen thinks.

I find flat ballet shoes at the bottom of the cupboard, and they change to fit me perfectly as I slide them on. I cross my arms and walk to the door, eyeing the hand scanner. I lift my hand and place it against the panel. It flashes purple before it goes red.

"Restricted access," a computer woman's voice exclaims.

Ah, smart alien man doesn't trust me yet. I knock the door twice, and it slides open as Zex lowers his hand from the scanner on the other side.

"Are you ready to see the ship?" he asks sweetly.

"No, I've changed my mind. I want to go to my room, and then I want you to leave," I say, and his eyes widen. "And no, I don't want to eat or see the rest of my prison."

The scanner told me I'm a prisoner, *basically*, so I'm going to act like one.

Screw you, big alien guy.

CHAPTER SIX

Pushing the white sheets away, I sit up on the bed and stare around my room like it might have changed. It hasn't, and neither has the pang of loneliness that I've never felt before. The silver chest of drawers sits right at the end of my bed, full of similar clothing in purples or silver or black. I did find my bag when Zex left me in this room, and I'm happy I have some of my normal clothes, but I have to admit the clothes in the drawers are comfier than anything I have ever owned. The rest of the room is plain, just white tiled flooring and white walls. The wall near the bathroom is all glass, so I can see the great expanse of outer space as this ship passes through it.

As a kid, I used to stare into space and look at all the dying stars, wondering how something that is dying a long death can be so beautiful. I remember my mum telling me I was too serious for a child and I should just see the beauty in the stars, not think about what they truly are.

But I could never do that. I always had to look beyond the outward appearance of everything and dig to see what was hidden beneath.

Dad said I saw the world with open eyes, and mum said I saw too much bad in the world and never looked for the good.

But mostly...I saw that was them. Dad was a wise man, but mum dealt with so much bad that she had to look desperately for the good. And she knew the good was hard to come by, so she became a little jaded and didn't let many get close to her.

I like to think I'm a bit of them both mixed into one.

I quickly shower and get dressed in a silver top and black trousers before grabbing a pillow. I place it down in front of the glass and sit on it, looking over space. It truly is wonderful and beautiful though. And under less *about to be a breeder for a big alien man* circumstances, I might feel lucky.

I hear the door slide open behind me, but I don't look back as no doubt poor Zex walks in. He has come every day for the last three days, but he isn't who I want to see. I'm not leaving this room until he comes to see me. Nope.

"This has gone on for far too long. How are you not starving?" Zex asks, coming over to me and sitting at my side. "You must be hungry by now."

"Starving is normal for us on Earth. I can go longer than three days without food," I inform him.

"We don't know each other, but I can tell you are stubborn and most likely will stay here until you pass out," he says and sighs. "But I would like to be your friend, and part of being a friend is telling you to leave this room and eat. There is a whole ship full of people outside this door."

"I will not leave to become some breeder for a man who won't even come to me," I answer. "I will not be forced into anything because of The Mates Lottery."

"No one on this ship will force you to do anything. *Especially* not him," Zex firmly tells me. "I have known Rox since we were young, and he is a good man. A good warrior who has saved my life at least a dozen times and saved a lot of lives when he didn't need to. Never once has he looked for anything for himself, and he never wanted to be involved in The Mates Lottery until he came to Earth and something changed. I believe he will make a good mate for you, and you for him, but this is not how you should start it."

"Do you have a mate?" I question, avoiding the subject.

"Yes, back home," he tells me with a kind smile. "And a little girl who is just over one. I have not met her in person yet. We are returning from a one and half year trip."

"I'm sorry she was born without you there," I say.

"My mate's pregnancy was a huge surprise. We never expected to be gifted a miracle," he says, beaming with joy. "Especially not on our mating night, the day before I left for this mission. Our daughter is a gift from the goddess, that I am sure of."

He returns to looking back out at space, and I watch him for a moment. He may look so different to me, his green skin making that obvious, but he's kinda human in how he talks, how he feels, I imagine. I guess the main issue for me on this ship is that I don't know who to trust or how to trust anyone. "Why are your women mostly infertile?"

"If you get to know your own intended mate, perhaps he will tell you," he responds with a playful smirk. "I will tell you we are from the planet Strixa, and that is where we are heading home to."

"But nothing else?" I question, and he shakes his head with amusement in his eyes.

"Come with me," he says as he stands, and when I don't move, he sighs. "Please. My role in life is to heal those who need help, and I can't stand to see you suffering. Let me help you."

"Fine, but then we come right back here," I mutter, giving in a little just for Zex. I feel sorry for him... I don't want to get him in trouble.

And I may or may not be starving.

But I won't admit that.

He smiles and nods once. I follow him out of my room and into a large corridor, which has only three other doors, judging by the panels on the walls. At the end of the corridor is an open door with a pad on the side of the wall. This leads to a big common area, which I remember coming through last time. It's full of white couches and seats, and is otherwise pretty empty. Right in the middle is a table with tablets, and automated piano music infuses the room just like last time I walked through. We head past the door to the medical bay and to another open door. I step in after Zex, and the chatter of the room fills my ears right away as does the smell of cooked food. My stomach rumbles as I take in the busy room full of straight tables and many, many people with green skin.

I spot another human woman in the strings of people who don't look my way, but she does. She has pitch-black hair and can't be much older than I am at twenty-two. A purple-skinned man with brown hair sits super close to her, and she looks away from me to kiss his cheek. I keep my eyes down as I follow Zex to a line of people waiting. We eventually get to the front where I am handed a tray full of roasted potatoes and chicken, as well as a chocolate cake pot and a bottle of water. My mouth waters as Zex grabs his own tray and nods his head at an empty table. I slide into the seat and don't waste any time digging into the food. *Gods, this is heaven.* Every mouthful seems to taste better than the last, and I'm so lost in my food that I barely notice as a guy sits down next to me.

"So this must be the new MLW?" the green-skinned guy asks Zex. *Mates Lottery Winner. Of course.* I look at him out of the corner of my eye as I eat my food. His skin tone is lighter than Zex's—and Khirrox's, I would bet—and he has deep brown hair that is all messy in a cute way. He playfully grins at me as Zex answers.

"Yes. This is Darcie," he introduces me.

"Nice to meet you, Darcie," he tells me, offering his hand for me to shake. I put my fork and knife down and take his hand. "I'm Strad Bheidiets, best friend to moody-ass Rox and here to protect you if you need it as I am a proud member of Rox's guard."

He lets my hand go as I try to figure out who he is talking about. "Rox is Khirrox?"

"Yes, but those close to him call him Rox," he explains to me. "You've really put him in a bad mood. Training is shit. Can you cheer him up for me?"

He flashes me a flirty, playful grin.

"No." I scowl, going back to my food. Surprisingly, Strad just laughs, and even Zex chuckles a little bit.

"They are as stubborn as each other, aren't they?" Strad asks Zex. He only nods with a smile he can't hide. *Dicks.*

"Well, it's good to meet you, Darcie. Let me know if you need anything," Strad tells me as I finish off my food, and I sense he is evaluating me.

"Like a one-way ride back to Earth?" I hopefully ask, and he only laughs as he gets up and walks out the room. *I will take that as a nope.*

"Why don't we take a walk around the ship?" Zex asks me. "And please do not ask more men to take you home. They may get the wrong idea, and then Rox will punch them or worse."

"Am I allowed to walk around with my restricted access?" I sarcastically question.

"Your access is restricted because you are not trusted yet. Hiding in your room does not help my judgment of you and your intentions towards my people." Rox's voice makes me freeze, and the familiar feeling settles in my gut as I turn my head back to see him right behind me. "Zex, you are dismissed. I will take Darcie on her tour."

Zex gets up quickly and smiles at me before leaving me alone with alien dickhead over here.

"Are you not going to say please?" I question, standing up from the table and crossing my arms.

"No," he all but snaps, and I smile sweetly at him.

"Say please, and I will go with you. If not, I'm going back to my room and staying in there for another three days," I reply. The tic in his jaw pulses as he stares me down, and even though people carry on talking in the room, I almost feel like it goes silent as we hold each other's gaze. I will not give in.

"Please," he grits out, and I grin.

"Look how easy that was! Come on then, big guy. Show me around," I say, stepping to his side and patting his shoulder. He grumbles something under his breath before placing his hand on my lower back and accompanying me out of the room.

I think I just won that round.

Big alien man: 0. Small human: 1.

CHAPTER SEVEN

"These are the warrior training grounds," Rox explains to me, pointing at a set of double doors that actually look like doors compared to the moving wall things everywhere else. Nothing but grunts and swearing can be heard from the other side of the door, and Rox quickly steers me away from that room.

Nothing but grunts and swearing can be heard from the other side of the door.

"What does finxu mean?" I ask, thinking my inner ear translator made a mistake.

The tips of Rox's ears almost turn a rosy color as he clears his throat. His eyes sweep quickly over my body.

"Er, I can not say," he chokes out and quickly

steers me away from that room. So far I've learnt this ship is huge, and I'm going to get lost for sure. It's hard to take in everything Rox is showing me as we go along. "If you need me in the day, I spend the mornings in there and the evenings in my private quarters."

"This ship is insane," I admit, feeling a little overwhelmed.

"Can I show you the best part of this ship? The reason that it is mine?" he asks me, and I nod. His hand finds my lower back once more and guides me to the door to the left of his private rooms. He opens the door with his hand on the pad, and we head inside to a plain circular room. He lets me go and picks up two large triangle-shaped pins that are clipped on the wall.

"May I?" he asks, and I nod. He steps close to me and presses the pin onto my top by my collarbone. A strange purple liquid covers all my skin from my head down and makes a bubble around my head. "This will keep you warm and make you able to breathe outside the ship. There is a force field about five metres around every inch of the ship, which makes it easy for us to go out into, even in space in mid-flight. I can survive about five minutes outside while in the force field, but you, as a human, would only survive possibly two minutes without one of these. Neither of us would survive for a second outside the force field, even in these suits."

He presses a pin to his shirt, and the same purple liquid shimmers as it covers him up to his neck and makes a bubble around his head.

"We are going outside? You're taking me into space?" I question with wide eyes. He offers me his hand, and pushing my nerves aside, I take his large hand, which makes mine look so small. Why I trust him, I don't know. I've never really trusted a guy before, let alone a huge green alien one. He leads me to the other side of the small room and enters in a code on a touchpad. Two little magnet-looking things float off the wall and clip themselves onto Rox's back and mine. A long metal chain extends from them to the wall, and then the door slides open and my feet leave the floor, letting us float. I feel a tiny bit cold as Rox pulls me out into open space around the ship.

"This is amazing," I whisper as tears fill my eyes. I never, ever could have dreamed of something as incredible as this is. My heart soars as we float outside the ship, and I try to spin around. Rox lets my hand go, and he effortlessly flips himself over. I copy, with far more effort, and he smiles for a moment as I awkwardly straighten.

Heck me, he has a sexy smile.

Soon enough he pulls me back into the ship, and the door shuts. My feet slam onto the floor, and I wobble a little, but Rox grabs my elbow to straighten me.

"Thank you! I've always dreamed of flying on a plane, like in the movies, and then jumping out with a parachute. But no one does that on Earth anymore, and we didn't have the money for the things they did have. But that felt like flying! That was amazing!" I say, meaning every word as I pull the pin off my shoulder and the suit disappears.

"Any time you wish, we can do that," he tells me, putting the clip back on the wall. "It is perfectly safe as long as you are with me or possibly one of my guards."

"Got it," I reply, walking out of the door. "No solo missions."

We head back out into the corridor, which is now empty, and the ship is rather silent. It's peaceful almost, nothing quite like I expected an alien ship to be like.

"I am sorry for my frosty greeting. You have to understand some Lottery winners do not want to be here at all and have killed in the past to try and escape. The doors were locked while Zex and I decided on your character. But I believe I have been harsh with you," he tells me. I have heard stories of the Lottery winners gone wrong. Some even kill themselves before being picked up, or their families kill them, not wanting them to have a life in space.

"If you tried to take me by force, I would kill you," I tell him with a sweet smile. "I may seem nice... but I will defend myself."

"I would never take a woman who did not want me. I have killed men for such acts," he sternly replies. "You are free to travel the communal areas of the ship if you wish, and know nothing bad will happen to you."

"Thank you," I tell him, strangely warming up to him.

"Would you like to join me for dinner tonight?" Rox's invite takes me by surprise as we carry on walking.

"That sounds too much like a date, so nope," I answer. He stops and turns towards me.

"Would a date be such a terrible thing?" he asks, his deep and seductive voice suggesting I should say yes. Dammit.

"We don't know each other," I say, pointing out the obvious. "And I would not make you a good breeder/wife/whatever you are looking for."

"Good thing I'm not looking for a breeder," he replies, stepping closer, and his minty and masculine scent washes over me and makes my knees weak. *How did I not notice how good he smells?* Rox places a finger under my chin and lifts my head up to meet his eyes. "I'm looking for a mate to protect with my life."

I feel his words like a lightning bolt smacking into my body and bringing every part of it alive.

"You've got the romance part of the equation sorted then," I nervously reply, my mouth feeling dry.

His eyes search mine. "You're not ready to accept this, and I understand that. I wish to court you if you will give me a chance."

I step away, needing to breathe, but it feels impossible when I'm so close to him. I turn away and cross my arms as I look out the nearby window. "No dating. I'm sorry, I'm just not what you wanted."

"Why did you enter The Mates Lottery if you didn't want this?" he questions, and I hear the disappointment in his voice. Surprisingly, it hurts something inside me, almost like I can feel his pain as my own.

Which is insane.

"My youngest sister, Alice, is very sick. Has been

since she was a baby, and we needed the money for medicine. I never expected to be picked," I truthfully answer because he deserves to know.

"I see," he replies, stepping to my side. "This all makes some sense now."

"Will you send me home then?"

He looks down at me, something crossing his expression I can't read. "If in eight months when we get to Strixa, you truly still wish to go home, I will allow it. I will send you home with enough money to live a comfortable life."

"Why would you do that?" I ask, feeling confused.

"I do not like to see suffering, and I see it in your eyes. It hurts me," he eventually answers. "Now that is discussed, I will leave you alone, and I will go have it made possible for you to move around the ship with no restrictions. My private rooms are just at the end of this corridor if you change your mind."

I sadly smile at him, and he bows his head before turning around and walking away. Strangely, I miss him...and I don't even know anything about him at all. I force myself to turn around and walk away, back to my rooms, even when I feel strangely conflicted about my choice to refuse his date. It's no more his fault than it is mine that we are stuck together, and what could the harm be in a date?

"S-orry!" a boy exclaims nearby, and I walk around the corridor to see a familiar human boy picking up empty plates off the floor where he must have dropped them. An alien man is storming away down the corridor, and I roll my eyes. I lean down and pick up a few plates and hand them to the boy as he straightens the tray he had them on.

"You!" I whisper as I realise why the boy looks so familiar. His skinny frame looks fuller, his dusty brown hair is washed and cut now, not covering his eyes like it was last time. He is pretty cute all cleaned up. "Do you remember me? What are you doing on here?"

"I re-mber," he tells me, not quite sounding right but close. "Rox help me. Giv-e ma job."

Shock leaves me silent, and I wordlessly help him pick up the remaining plates.

"What's your name?"

"Mick," he answers with bright cheeks before he runs off back to his work. Rox saved him after seeing me help him escape in that alleyway. *Why would he do that?*

If he did it for me, that wouldn't make any sense as he didn't find out I was his mate-to-be until a few days later, which means he just helped Mick because he *could*, making him a good person. I actually admire that he did that. It must have been a lot of trouble to convince the human government to let Rox take the kid on board.

Yet he still did it.

I turn around and walk around the corridor and right up to the door leading to Rox's private area. I knock twice and wait. A few moments later, Rox opens the door up, and he looks damn surprised to see me.

"I accept your date. What time were you thinking for dinner?"

CHAPTER EIGHT

Brushing out the last of the knots in my towel-dried hair, I nearly jump when someone knocks on the door from the other side.

"One second!" I shout as I scramble to gather my clothes and pull them on. I'm sure I look a right mess when I open the door using the touchpad, and the human woman I saw from earlier is standing in front of me. Her black hair is pulled into a tight ponytail, and her tight clothes are the same material that I have on, but she has killer high heels on her feet rather than the flats I've chosen.

She is still very beautiful. On her arms are strange tattoos in swirls that shimmer purple almost when I look directly at them and then disappear when I look away.

"Hello. I thought I'd come and introduce myself and see if you wanted a friend. Humans like us have to stick together, right?" she says, but her thick accent is unfamiliar to me. "My name is Marnie Hexin, and I was a Lottery winner three years ago."

"Nice to meet you, Marnie. I'm Darcie Jackson," I say and step to the side so she can come in. She grins and steps into my room, walking over to and sitting in the small chair where I just was. I decide to sit on the end of the bed, facing her. "Why are you on this ship then?"

"Oh, my mate is part of Rox's personal guard, and I didn't want to leave him. This mission wasn't counted as extremely dangerous, so he said I could come," she explains to me. "I'm sure once you and Rox are mated, you will understand how hard it is to be away from them for a long time."

Not knowing how to answer that, I change the subject. "So what is the planet of Strixa like?"

"Beautiful and peaceful. I miss it more than Earth, that is for sure," she tells me. "Though my life on Earth wasn't all that great in comparison."

"Where abouts are you from?"

"The English colony, although more Welsh by blood. I lost my parents young, and I was lucky to be taken in by an adoptive family," she explains to me. "What about you?"

"America, near what used to be Orlando. My parents died five years ago, and it was just me and my four sisters. I'm finding it hard to be away from them, and I'm worried," I admit, and her eyes soften.

"Well, I don't have any friends or family. Why don't we be that for each other?" she asks. Oddly, it warms my heart.

"Yes, I'd like that," I answer, and she smiles back at me.

"As your friend, I have to comment on how lucky you are. Most women on Earth would die to be chosen for a mate of a prince!" she tells me, and I freeze. *Prince?* "I mean, I know he isn't the next in line for the throne, but my mate, Xemak, told me he is far more respected. Plus, the throne of Strixa is never given to the next-born heir, but it's who wins some kind of ancient warrior battle."

"He's a prince?" I whisper. "Why the hell would he want me as a mate?"

"Don't put yourself down. You're beautiful and strong-willed. Rox has always bossed every single person on this ship around, and he couldn't do that with you. You're perfect for him," she suggests. "You will challenge him, make him better, and if one day he becomes king, you will be a beautiful queen."

"Queen? Me?" I chuckle. "I don't see that *ever* happening. I don't have a royal bone in my body."

She laughs, standing up and walking to me. "I think you will steal the hearts of every person on Strixa just by being with Rox. He is loved on Strixa. You're likeable. I would happily call you my queen, so don't worry, others will."

"You just want to keep me as a friend because the alien women are weird," I point out with an eyebrow overly arched, only making her laugh more.

"Oh yeah, they are strange to us but normal for them. There aren't any other women on this ship but me and you. They don't like to ever put their mates or women at risk," she explains to me, a dark shadow crossing over her eyes. "After what happened, I can understand it."

"What *did* happen?" I ask, and she walks over, sitting next to me on the bed and looking down.

"About thirty-some years ago, an unknown race of beasts that almost look like dragons to us attacked all the five planets at once. Their blood poisoned the waters, making them undrinkable, and they took most of the women and children. Everyone fought back, of course, but they just disappeared one day," she whispers, and my heart hurts for all the people who must have lost someone. "They call it the Dragonmir war, as that's what they call the creatures. The water was drunk by a lot of the women and men on the planets, and later on they figured out they had a big fertility problem, which must have been caused by the invaders' blood in the waters."

"That's why they trade with Earth for water and fertile women," I mutter, rubbing my hands together. "It's all so sad. Have the Dragonmir race ever attacked again?"

"No, they have long disappeared. Along with most of the women and children," she tells me. "There was a baby princess, Rox's sister, who was also taken. They pray to their goddess of life for their safety every day. You should come. Their version of a chapel is on the top level of the ship, number eight, and you can find the lift by the training rooms. Tomorrow, two p.m. I know Rox is a big believer, as he wears her symbol as a necklace."

"I'll meet you there," I say. "Actually, what time is it now?"

She lifts her wrist, where she has an old watch. "It's nearly seven. Wanna walk to the dining hall, I bet Xemak is looking for me."

"I have a date, but I'm walking that way. Let's go," I tell her, and she steps back, shaking her head.

"You can't have a date with a prince wearing that. No way," she exclaims, grabbing my hand and dragging me to the door. "My room isn't far. I'm princessing you up, girl."

Should I be scared?

———

"YOU LOOK DIVINE, DARCIE." Rox's comment washes over me as I stand outside his door in a pale silver dress that clings to my body at the stop. The satin material wraps around my body with a sweetheart neckline and criss-crosses on my upper back. My caramel blonde hair is wrapped up in a messy bun, a few strands brushing against my neck. I gulp as I take in Rox in a smart white shirt tucked into tight black trousers. A few buttons on his white shirt are undone, the stark contrast of white and the deep green colour of his skin oddly beautiful. His sleeves are rolled up, making him look like a sexy alien boss instead of the sexy alien prince he actually is.

"So do you," I reply and resist the urge to smack myself in the head with my hand. I suck at flirting. He laughs and steps aside for me to walk in. After a ten-minute argument with my new bestie, Marnie, we agreed I could keep my flat shoes instead of any heels. My feet make almost no sound as I step onto the thick cream carpet that covers Rox's massive living quarters. The room is sectioned with half walls, where one part has his giant black bed with black sheets, and above the bed is a painting of shooting stars littered across a black sky. There is also a huge dark wooden piano taking up another side, which surprises me. His living area with several black couches and a glass coffee table is in the middle, and next to it is a long dark wooden dining table set up for two. Bright purple flowers that remind me of roses—but they are sparkling and far prettier—are in a vase in the middle of the table, and there is a section of different foods spread out for us to pick from.

"What flowers are those?" I ask Rox as we walk over to the table. "And do you like dark rooms by any chance?"

"To answer your second question first, yes I do," he says, holding out a chair for me. I sit down, and his fingers graze across the back of my neck, making me shiver. He walks around the table to his side, leaving us facing each other. Placing his elbows on the table, he links his fingers, and heck even his forearms are sexy. *Head outta the gutter, Darcie.* "To answer your first, they are called Lumina flowers, and they are from my planet. They have long lifespans and are known for good luck. I always make sure my ship has some onboard."

"Like sailors and horseshoes from Earth. They always have a horseshoe on board, and the sailors must touch it before they take off. They also believe a woman on board is bad luck, which is total rubbish," I reply with a laugh, and he chuckles with me before he waves his hand at the food.

"Help yourself, Darcie," he suggests. I do just that, piling my plate with food, and he waits until I stop before picking his own plate up to fill. The moment I take a bite of the pork and potatoes, I'm in love.

We eat in silence, not an awkward kind either like I expected it might be. We are strangely comfortable. "May I ask where your name comes from? Does it have special meaning on Earth?"

I smile. "Not exactly, no. My mum loved a film or book called *Pride and Prejudice*. My name comes from the last name of a character in that film. But slightly different."

"I will watch this movie," he nods, and I try not to

chuckle at the idea of this big green alien warrior watching a historical romance movie.

"What about your name?"

"It means blessed prince in my language," he answers.

"Makes sense, considering you are one," I reply with a raised eyebrow.

"Ah, I see someone has been talking to you," he replies with an amused tint in his eyes.

"I'm very likeable, apparently," I answer.

"That you are, Darcie," he agrees, and somehow the room becomes thick with tension once more. I look away, needing a moment to breathe, and scramble to come up with anything to change the subject.

"So, uh, tell me what it's like growing up as a prince?"

He waits until I look back to answer me. "After the Dragonmir war, which I assume you know about by now..." I nod and he continues, "everyone was highly protective of new children. I was one of the last babies born for a long time on Strixa. My brothers and I were overprotected in a sense, and finding Earth and the peace treaty was a lifeline for our people. As I'm sure it is the same for the other planets."

"Aren't you at war with two of them, if I remember right?" I question.

"Yes, we have active wars open with Tabrerth and Giea. They are quite barbaric planets, less advanced than we are, to say the least. The other two planets, we have a peace treaty with," he explains to me. "But less about war. It's a hard subject to speak on."

"Sure," I answer tightly, but I can't help but wonder if one or more of my sisters are on these planets, and I might never be able to see them again. I focus on my food, a weight settling on my chest that I can't seem to push off.

"Have I upset you?" Rox asks me, and I look up.

"Not you. I was just thinking of my sisters," I explain. "It isn't your fault."

"I am sorry you are separated from them," he tells me. "I have an older sister lost somewhere in space, and I can understand your grief. Family is so important."

"I'm glad we agree on that. There isn't anything I wouldn't do for my family and those I love," I tell him. Something akin to respect reflects in his eyes.

Taking a deep breath, I shake away the sadness that has settled over me. My eyes flick over to the piano. "Do you play?"

"Yes. Pianos have been part of our culture for many decades. I found it interesting Earth has the same interest in music as our race does. May I play you a song?" he asks.

"Okay!" I say, pushing my chair out as he stands with me. His hand flattens across my lower back as he leads me over to the piano. He sits down, and I sit next to him, his whole leg pressed against mine, and I can't focus on much other than how hot he feels. He doesn't waste time, expertly moving his fingers across the keys, and I find myself entranced in the music he plays, a song I have never heard before. I slowly rest my head against his shoulder, and he looks down at me, never stopping his song. I find his eyes, admiring how silver they are and how they are so easy to get lost in. *Gods, I sound like an old movie.* My gaze drifts down to his soft-looking lips, and I wonder what they would feel like against my own. Would they feel as good as they look? He stops playing, turning slightly to face me as I lift my head. He reaches forward, sinking his hand into my hair and cupping the back of my head.

I don't breathe as time slows down as he leans down and kisses me. Sharp waves of something slam through my body, bringing me to life in a way I have never felt as he tenderly kisses me, embracing me with every brush of his lips.

I know with utter certainty that I will be addicted to Rox for the rest of my life with just this one kiss.

That makes him so utterly dangerous.

"Sorry to interrupt, we have a problem with the prisoner. We need you." Strad's voice cuts through the haze, and Rox breaks the kiss, lowering his hand while his eyes burn with anger.

He stares at Strad over my shoulder, the tic in his jaw starting slightly before he nods. He looks back at me, and I'm certain I can feel his disappointment as my own.

"I must leave. You are more than welcome to wait—"

"No, I will go back to my room," I say, climbing off the seat. He reaches for me, but I step back quickly. What was I thinking? I can't fall for an alien prince. Not if I ever want to see my sisters again. "Thank you for a lovely night."

I rush out of the room, ignoring how every single inch of my heart begs me to go back.

CHAPTER NINE

I sneak through an open door, and the second I do, I realise I didn't need to sneak into the chapel at all. I was invited...but I feel like an outsider. I guess like I do throughout the ship, even when everyone is nice. I've never had to be around this many people, and the divide between me being human and them not is too clear. I'm thankful for Marnie. She makes it all seem a little less lonely and daunting. The room is quiet in that serene way a church always is even when it is full of people. In the centre of the dome-shaped room is a statue of a naked woman made of pure white glass. She has robes hanging over her shoulders, which fall down her back alongside her hair and pool at her feet. The woman is staring up at the top of the dome, her clear eyes bright even when they aren't alive. Around the statue are at least ten green aliens on their knees, their heads bowed down as they whisper something. I nearly jump when a hand lands on my shoulder, and I spin around to see Marnie and her mate, Xemak. She lowers her hand as I grin at her, and she nods her head to three spaces on the one side. I feel strangely nervous as I kneel on one of the red rugs laid out. I open my mouth to ask Marnie what we do next when a voice from my other side derails that thought.

"May I sit next to you?"

I turn to face Rox who stands over me, and immediately I'm lost for words. All I can think of is our kiss and how, starting right after that, I don't sense him like I used to do. I don't feel that smack in the chest when he is near...instead, I feel a sense of familiarity, of safety.

And nope. That just can't happen.

But my brain doesn't catch up as quickly as my hormones do, as I end up nodding.

Dammit. Plan "Avoid Sexy Alien Prince" is failing.

Rox kneels on a red rug right by mine, so ridiculously close that I can do nothing but breathe in whatever hot alien scent he has going on.

"Who are you praying for?" I whisper. "In fact,

who are *we* praying to? I don't know much about this goddess of life."

"Her name is Vyuna, and we refer to her as the goddess of the Harvest," he softly tells me, almost like he is singing me a lullaby. "They say Vyuna and her nameless mate created the universe for each other. Every planet was a gift, and each gift was better than the last. Their love spanned thousands, if not millions, of years until Vyuna grew bored with the worlds that had no life. In her misery, her mate stabbed himself in the heart and flew around the planets, bleeding life into the worlds for her to love."

"That's so sad," I whisper back.

Rox sorrowfully smiles. "The words written on the base of every statue of Vyuna are 'We create worlds for those we love,' and I believe her mate did the right thing. He could not see his mate in pain, and he knew the only way to fix her life was to give her what she wants."

"Was Vyuna happy with the life she created?"

He looks up at the statue this time. "They say she died at the same time as her mate, unable to stand life without him in it. They loved each other deeply, and it was the first real mating. Now, many people can mate, find those who are destined for each other."

"They were lucky then. Many spend their whole

lives looking for love and never finding it," Marnie adds in, and until she spoke, I forgot she was even there. I nod and look up at the statue.

I don't speak my prayer out loud, but I do pray for my sisters. For wherever they are in the universe and that I might get a chance to see them once again.

I wait for a long time before getting up and high-tailing my arse out of the room. The corridor is empty as I wait for the elevator, but soon he is at my side, and I know it's him without having to look.

"I have the feeling you are avoiding me," he softly comments.

Biting down on my lip, I stare at the elevator doors, willing them to open. "And I have no idea where you would get such an idea."

His lips twitch, and I stare at them for a moment too long as he notices, his eyes dropping to my own lips. Desperate to change the subject and cut into the tension building in the small space, I blurt out whatever I can. "How many battles have you been in? Have you always been a warrior?"

The elevator doors open before he can answer, and we step in. Rox presses the button, his arm brushing against mine as he reaches for it, and I swear I feel the brief contact all the way down my body. "I have won seven hundred and six battles with my men, and I would trust every single one of my guard with my life. We all trained together, and never once did they treat me as a prince, they treated me as their brother, and respect was earnt, not given."

"I've only met Zex and Strad, but I've seen five others. What was your worst battle?" I ask as the elevator gets to the main floor and we both step out. Rox waves a hand towards one of the white sofas in the common area, and I walk over, sitting down with him against my better judgment. He sits next to me, his thigh pressed against mine like he just needs to be touching me.

And I don't hate that.

"Strad and I went on a solo mission to Giea to save five kidnapped women. Two of them were pregnant, and we knew a big guard could not sneak onto the planet like we could. When we finally got there, they had killed all of the women and only kept the two babies. They were being cared for by a Gie woman, and she would not give up the babies. I had to kill her, and it was a difficult choice. We rescued the babies, and they have homes with their fathers and extended family on Strixa." He looks down as he speaks, and I can hear the guilt in his voice.

"You did the right thing. It's not okay for a baby to be taken from its family," I tell him firmly.

"It was difficult because the Gie woman loved those babies like they were her own and likely had nothing to do with the kidnapping and killing of their mothers. But she would not come with us or give the babies up," he tells me. "I understand the pain many suffer in longing for a child when there are so few. It makes me angry that your planet treats its children so badly."

"They treat everyone badly. Earth is a mess, but it was home," I tell him. "Thank you for talking with me. I feel like I know you better now."

"And somehow I have learnt nothing about you. Tell me something, anything," he asks as I stand up off the sofa.

"I like you, and it freaks me out. So yes, I'm avoiding you," I blurt out, swiftly turning around and practically running away.

I'm a total coward.

But falling for an alien prince just cannot happen.

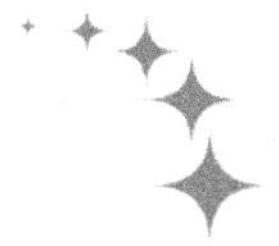

CHAPTER TEN

The soothing sound of the piano sings its way into my ears, but the upbeat, almost fun song is not one I expected to hear in the middle of the ship. It reminds me of a song from home that I can't remember the name of, but I'm sure it was played for children. I slow down, and turn away from the cafeteria where I was heading and follow the music to the hallway. Rox is sitting on the piano stool, playing the music, and at his side is Mick. He looks so tiny in comparison, but his whole face is lit up as Rox is clearly playing for him. Even though Mick looks small, he looks so much healthier than he ever has. Every time I see him on the ship, I just want to hug him and cheer that he has this chance in life.

And every time, I want to kiss Rox for saving him.

I stay in the corner of the room, even as the song ends and Mick claps for a long time, even letting out a little cheer.

"My ma-ma like mus-ic," Mick quietly tells Rox, and my heart hurts for the little boy so much.

"I will play for you whenever you want, Mick. What did happen to your parents?" Rox gently asks him.

"Mon-ey gone. Foo-d go-nn-e. Ba-d men c-ome," he replies. His jumbled up speech is actually getting so much better than it was and just about under-standable. Every inch of me wants to run and hug Mick, to tell him how sorry I am that his parents were killed. His story isn't far off from what a lot of people on Earth experience now. I instantly think of Isabelle, of how she is alone on that planet with nothing to protect her anymore.

I miss her so much.

"Where we are going, money and food will never cost someone their life. You will love Strixa, it is known as the Everlong Forest by my people. The trees protect us, and they will protect you. I am sorry for your past, but do not let it beat you. Remember your parents, and honour them by becoming a great man," Rox tells him and pats his back. "Everyone has a past, a bad moment in their life they must overcome. This is yours, and I am certain you will overcome it in time."

"Than-k y-ou for sa-ving me," Mick tells Rox, and I smile as Rox ruffles his hair. I even see Rox's cheek look a little darker green, and I imagine that means he is embarrassed. I get that feeling about him. He is a guy who does not like to be known as the one who saved the day, a hero without a cape, and all that.

"How about we get going to dinner? There is a girl I want to see there," Rox asks, and Mick nods with a big grin. I stay put as they both make their way to the cafeteria, and my heart feels like it's swelling with how cute and sweet Rox actually is.

Yes, he looks like a sexy but fierce warrior, but underneath it all? He is so much more than what it first seems like.

And oh does that make him so much more dangerous for me.

I cross my arms, lost in thought as I turn around and head back to my room. I get down the corridor and come to a stop, seeing Marnie and her mate kissing in the corridor. They are both clueless to my existence, giggling like teenagers as they kiss and he tickles her. The connection they have is something worth dying for. I know that, I can see it is something so special. To have someone in your life you can trust completely and love more than you thought you could ever love someone.

I leave them to it, sneaking past and straight to my room. Even though I can't really personalise a room, I feel like this place is so much more me now. My favourite blanket is across the white bedsheets, and I've done a few drawings of space and the planets we have passed. They are taped to the wall next to the drawings of my sisters I have done. I stare at the drawings of Chloe and Isabelle, a memory I have of them both coming back drunk from their first party. Sav was so mad, but they both couldn't stop giggling because they had dragged the cow into the living room and it was eating the plant we used to have.

The next morning, it took all five of us to drag the poor cow out of the house and back into the field. But even despite all that, it was the funniest day.

For a moment, I wonder what my sisters would think of Rox, or even more, what mum and dad would have made of him. I think Sav and mum would have welcomed him with open arms when she saw the good in his eyes, but Dad and Chloe would have been suspicious. Alice and Isabelle would have sectioned me for going insane, I'm sure of it.

But it wouldn't have mattered to me. I feel defensive of him now and I would have sold him to my family no matter what.

Gods, it's so much more than that. I don't know how I'm going to walk away when this is all over.

And if I can't walk away from him, then I'm leaving my sisters to fend for themselves...so either way, this trip only ends in heartbreak.

CHAPTER ELEVEN

Turns out I'm a master at one very important thing: avoiding one sexy alien prince like my life depended on it. It's been a month since our date, with our short but addictive kiss, and I have managed to escape being alone with Rox at any chance I have gotten except for a few times in the chapel where I actually love going now. I get the feeling he is getting annoyed, but I don't know what to say to him, now that I've admitted I like him. And I do. If he was someone I met on Earth, I'd be in bed with him by now and hoping he wasn't a total asshole like most men. I'd always planned to settle down when I was older, have a few kids and just a general life like I saw my parents have.

This alien mating thing was never part of my life plan.

"Darcie, how are you today?" Zex asks me, falling into step with me as I walk down the corridor that leads past the training rooms and to the stairs. His white doctor robes are super bright this morning, and he looks happy.

"Rather bored, if I'm being honest," I say, crossing my arms as I stop before the training room doors. The usual sounds of grunting and swear words drift through the doors, and I realise this is one of the rooms I haven't been in yet. Zex follows my gaze.

"I wouldn't recommend exploring this room. The men train roughly," Zex warns me, and I smile at him.

"Do you train?" I ask, running my eyes over his muscular body. He isn't as ripped as Rox, but he has more of a swimmer's body. "Or is it not something you have to do as a healer."

"I'm a personal healer of a prince. Training is mandatory of anyone around him," he explains.

"So...that means I need to be trained if I wanna stay?"

"Women do not need to learn such defensive skills. We will always protect our women, you included, even if you don't want to stay." He waves off my suggestion. Not in a patronising way, just in a sense he never thought about women learning to fight before.

"Right, so, no women train at all on Strixa? There are no females in your armies?" I question. When he nods, anger fills me for them. Women are *not* tiny little fragile figurines that need to be protected. We can learn to fight and even beat these sexist alien assholes. I hold my head high, ignoring Zex calling for me as I quickly walk through the doors and come to a halt.

Oh my gosh. Shirtless sexy aliens everywhere. *Hello!*

I don't know where to look first. At least twenty alien men are dotted around the giant room, which is full of obstacles, with a huge square pool of cold-looking water in the centre. Around the pool are large flat hills, and from the ceiling hangs ropes with rubber circle handles hanging off them. The side walls are littered with climbing holds that go all the way up to the ceiling.

"Darcie, I really think we should leave—" I stop listening to Zex as I see *him.* My heart pangs hard in my chest as I spot Rox climbing up the one hill like a monkey. *Albeit, a really hot shirtless alien monkey.* My mouth feels dry as his arms flex while he grabs the top of the hill and pulls himself up with one hand. He leans down and runs fast, jumping off the hill. I take a step forward like I could save him from the fall somehow, but he doesn't fall at all. He catches one of the hanging ropes and uses his body to swing himself from rope to rope until he gets to the last one.

And then he frigging lets it go.

He turns himself over, mid-air, and dives head-first into the cold water. I run to the edge, ignoring the whispers of the men around me who have stopped to stare. The seconds drift into minutes where he doesn't come back up, and I start to panic.

"Rox!" I all but scream, looking down into the water and not seeing him. Moments later he breaks out of the water, staring up at me and brushing his dark hair out of his eyes with a playful grin.

"You look concerned. Is there something wrong?" he asks me with amusement twinkling in his eyes. When I narrow my eyes back at him, he chuckles and places his arms on the edge of the pool. He pulls himself out and stands upright in front of me, and all I can focus on is his glistening chest and the way the water droplets drip down between his six-pack.

Focus, Darcie.

"I came here to learn how to protect myself," I state, my hands falling to my hips.

He smirks, stepping closer, and I suck in a deep breath. "I protect you. You do not need to learn."

"But I want to," I answer, holding my head high. "You can't always be at my side, and if I choose to go back to Earth, then I will need to learn."

"No matter where you are in the universe, I will protect you, Darcie," he softly tells me, reaching up and cupping my cheek with his damp hand.

"No one has ever said anything like that to me before," I whisper back, knowing my cheeks must be burning red at this point.

"If you didn't avoid me, you would learn the extent of my care for you," he suggests, and I grin.

"I still want to learn to fight. You haven't swayed me," I mumble back.

"Stubborn little Earthling," he murmurs, his eyes drifting down to my lips for a moment. I run my tongue across my dry lips on instinct.

"So is that a yes?" I ponder. He sighs and drops his hand. Rox surprises me when he leans forward and kisses my forehead, the soft and loving gesture leaving me speechless.

"Strad, come here," he calls, and I turn around as Strad jogs over to us, winking at me.

"I'm trusting you to teach Darcie some basic training moves," he says, never taking his eyes off me. "And in return, Darcie, you will not avoid me any longer."

"Deal, as long as Marnie can learn with me. If she wants to," I say, holding my hand out. Rox smiles and takes my hand, but instead of shaking it, he lifts my hand up and kisses my knuckles.

"Always negotiating, my little Earthling. Deal," he tells me, letting my hand go. "I am due to have a conference call back home, but I will come back later today to see your progress."

"Thank you," I tell him. He nods and walks to Strad's side. I can't hear what he tells Strad, but whatever it is, it makes him pale.

"Come on then, Darcie girl. We should start with sprints to build up your endurance." Strad steps up to me and points at a clear area behind the pool. I walk with him and glance at the door just as Rox disappears through it.

"What did Rox say to you?" I ask.

Strad laughs. "That if you get hurt, he is going to break my hands. And fair warning, he wasn't kidding. Save my hands and do as you're told today, Darcie."

"He wouldn't really—" I pause when I see how serious Strad is being.

"Rox is a warrior first, a prince second and a man last. But most of all, he is as protective of his mate as any warrior would be," he explains. "When I have a mate, I would die rather than see her hurt."

"Whoever you choose as a mate will be a lucky girl, Strad. You're a good guy," I tell him, and he looks down at me in slight confusion.

"Less a choice and more of a fate sent to us from our goddess of life," he reminds me. "Our markings tell us when our mate is near. Apparently humans can feel something akin to a shock, a feeling in their stomach or chest."

I pause mid-step. Was what I felt real? The shocked feeling when I first saw Rox and how it slowly wore away. I almost wonder what it would be like if I wasn't always near him like I am now. "What markings?"

"Rox has them on his back, if that is what you are asking, and here are mine." He lifts up his arms, and there on the back are strange dark green markings. Unless I was really close like I am now, I wouldn't even notice them. "Our mating happens differently than humans. We build a bond, and during sex, a mate bond can naturally happen if you are in love. It cannot be forced nor bred out of duty without love. A mating bond is a strong connection we all strive to find."

"And Rox thinks he can find that with me?"

"Yes," he answers. "The Mates Lottery takes your blood, correct?"

I can only nod. "There are markers in your blood that would make you compatible with one of our race. It seems you and Rox matched up somewhere. It was his first time entering."

"Why did he?"

"Why don't you ask him?" he counters, and I huff, stepping back. He laughs and waves me over to the mat. I may have gotten what I wanted, but somehow I still have a million questions more to ask my alien warrior.

***

"I'M DEAD, just leave me here. It's over for me," I dramatically gasp as I lie on the mat and suck in a long breath. Strad soon figured out I need to build endurance, but I also have strength in my arms, so he suggests rock climbing, and eventually I will be able to do most of the course they have in here. So for two hours, Strad the *demon* alien made me climb up and down the climbing frame.

"Come on up. Let's try some hand-to-hand combat," Strad suggests, offering me his hand.

"I hate you," I playfully tell him as I take his hand, and he pulls me to my feet.

"I will take over from here. Clear out the room, Strad," Rox says, and I am so worn out I hardly noticed him come into the room.

"Yes, sir," he cheekily replies to Rox, and Rox pats his shoulder as he passes him.

"You seem tired. We can rest if you wish," Rox asks me, crossing his large arms over his chest. Strad and all the guys in the room leave, and the only sound filling the space is the engine of the ship.

"I am fine. Teach me some hand combat please," I ask. Rox moves quickly behind me, almost like he didn't move at all, and his hands cover my own at my side.

"When someone gets you from behind, they are likely to be close. Do not use your hands, always use your head to knock them off, and then"—he spins me around to face him and lifts his neck—"one hard punch in the throat. This will give you a chance to run."

"Head and neck, got it," I reply, gulping at how close we are. He steps back, and I miss his closeness.

"Now punch my hand," he directs me, holding up his palm. Oddly, I feel strange about doing it, and I have to remind myself it's just training. I nod and lift my hand, punching his palm as hard as I can, and it hurts my knuckles.

"No." He takes my hand and folds it right, showing me how to hold it correctly. "Now try again, and you will see it does not hurt."

"Okay," I say and punch his palm one more time. "You're right, that didn't hurt half as bad!"

He smiles at me. "Rule one for a warrior: Learn how to punch correctly."

"So can we move onto swords now?" I ask, moving my eyes to the lines of swords on the wall. To my surprise, Rox bursts into laughter, and I can't help laughing with him. I step closer, placing my hand on his upper arm. "Is that a no?"

"I hate to refuse you, but first we master your body before mastering other weapons," he tells me and wraps his arms around my waist, like it's a natural thing to do. We are both chuckling as I lean up and kiss him, clearly shocking him still for a moment. Only a moment though, as he reacts quickly, kissing me deeper and picking me up as I plaster myself to his body. We kiss each other like long-lost lovers, and I can't get enough, wanting a bit more of him every second. He breaks the kiss first, and I stare at him as he rubs his thumb across my lips.

"What do you want, Darcie?"

"That's the problem...I don't know," I admit. "But I can't stop thinking about you."

"Mating, sex between us, would link our souls forever. I will not take you without you first understanding what it would mean," he tells me and lowers me, setting me back on my feet before letting go. "I will never be able to give you an Earth life, and I must live on Strixa. I am their prince."

"I know that. This all would be easier if you weren't a prince," I admit, and he sadly smiles.

"Vyuna never makes fate easy for us. Have a good evening, Darcie," he tells me, and his words hurt my heart.

And it hurts even more as I watch him walk away, because a small part of me thinks I'm meant to be at his side.

CHAPTER TWELVE

"May I borrow you for a few hours?" Rox asks, stepping into the common area where I am researching Strixa and everything I can find on the planet I am heading right to. I've basically found out the normal history stuff I already knew. Over thirty years ago, Strixa and the other four planets found Earth and made a peace treaty that has changed over the years. Strixa is widely known as the most advanced race in the galaxy. Its cities and ships are far more technologically advanced than other cultures and races. Even with the shared technology treaty, it has always seemed like Strixa knew far more.

"Yes, if you answer some new questions I have," I ask him, turning off the tablet and standing up. Rox's tight black ship clothes fit him so tightly it's like I can trace every bit of his muscular form all the way to his trousers which are a little looser. Shame.

Rox chuckles and offers me his arm. "Always negotiating. But yes."

With a big smile, I hook my arm in his and let him lead the way towards his living quarters, but we go past them towards the spacewalking place. "Are we spacewalking again?"

"No, but we are leaving the ship," he tells me, and I raise my eyebrows at him, which just seems to make him amused.

"Alone? Can the prince just leave the ship alone? And where could we go?" I ask as we go into the spacewalking space, and Rox leaves me on one side. He clips two long swords onto his back, both of them made of what looks like glowing green silver with the same markings I've seen on Rox's back drawn into them by hand. Rox covers the swords with a deep green cloak and pulls the hood up, reminding me of what he looked like when we first met.

For some reason, it makes my heart pound in my chest when he looks back at me, and I wonder if he is thinking exactly the same thing that I am.

"Here, it will be cold," he tells me, handing me a green cloak that matches his. I slide my arms through it, and Rox clips the silver clasp together at the front before stroking his hands down my arms and linking one of our hands. "You will be safe at my side, but please stay close."

"Promise," I tell him, seeking his eyes under the cloak and finding them almost instantly. "I always feel safe around you, Rox."

"It's because you always are," he replies, and a beep clicks somewhere nearby, making me nearly jump. He lightly chuckles and leads me over to a yellow circular patch that glows slightly.

"Hold your breath," he tells me, and just as I suck in a deep breath, the circle glows under our feet, and then it feels like I'm falling.

My stomach drops and my eyes slam shut just before a cold breeze blows across my face, and I open my eyes to see bright lights of a carnival of some kind, and we are off the ship. Multicoloured tents float in bubbles off the ground, lights blasting from each one in lots of different colours, and glitter sparkles in the air all around them. Loud music fills the air, as well as the sound of laughter, and I can see lots of people jumping from bubble to bubble like they can fly. I'm assuming the gravity is different here, as usually they couldn't jump like that. It's truly stunning.

"This is the Space Traveling Carnival, and they

travel from moon to moon, making camp and staying for weeks. We were passing, and I thought you might like to see it," Rox tells me. I'm speechless as I turn to him and jump, wrapping my arms around his shoulders and hugging him tightly. He holds me back as I breathe in how amazing he smells.

"Thank you! I'm so excited!" I say, letting go and stepping back, wanting to run to the carnival and see what is in all the tents.

Rox grins back at me and offers me his hand. I all but drag him to the first bubble and do a tiny jump. My tiny jump propels me up onto the bubble, which looks like it should pop, but it doesn't. I laugh with Rox, jumping from one to another until we get to the first tent.

"It's a fortune teller." Rox explains to me what the symbol means on the banner at the top of the red tent. "It's not a known power in the universe, but some people have unexplainable gifts. Like my mother, she can touch your skin and know if you are sick, or pregnant, or even broke a tiny bone in your toe."

"That's incredible," I say. "I can't wait to meet her. I know she must be lovely as she raised you, and you are—"

I pause and he laughs, not pushing me for the end of that sentence as my cheeks go bright red.

"Do you wish to go inside?"

"Yes," I reply, wanting to get out of this conversation however I can. We walk into the tent, which is small and cosy with a purple-skinned woman sitting on the floor on top of a yellow cushion. The woman has layers and layers of a shiny fabric covering her from head to toe and only a cut-out part around her eyes can be seen, as well as her hands resting on her lap. Her bright lilac eyes search us both before she waves at the top cushions about five feet away from her on the floor. Rox and I sit down, and I cross my legs as I watch the woman.

"It is an honour to have such royals in my tent," the woman states, her voice melodic. "A prince and princess is a rare sight indeed."

"How do you know this?" Rox demands, sounding tense.

"I'm not a princess," I tell her, covering Rox's knee with my hand.

"You will be a princess for a short while and a queen for a lifetime if Vyuna has her way," the woman tells us. "My name is Cherisa, Darcie Jackson. Do you have a question for me?"

A little speechless, I look to Rox, and he nods

once. "I want to know if my sisters will be okay. Do I need to save them? Will I ever see them again?"

"That was more than one question, but I will tell you one answer that I see. Your sisters will each need saving, each more than the last, but it is not you who will save them. Their fates are woven with another, much like yours is," she tells me and closes her eyes. "I see you all. I see your fate, and the stars are watching, sweet princess. They will guide you home."

"Thank you," I whisper, wiping a stray tear away. "So they aren't dead?"

"I cannot tell you anymore," she softly replies. "Vyuna gifted me, but I have my limits. I will not charge for this, but know we will see each other again one day."

"Thank you," Rox tells her as we both stand up.

"Yes, thank you," I say and look up at Rox. When I glance back, the woman is gone, and the tent is empty.

"How about we try something more fun next time?" Rox asks as we get outside. I nod, pushing back thoughts of my sisters and jumping up the bubbles to the next tent, which is green and a lot bigger. Above the door is a sign that looks like a duck inside a planet.

"This is a good one," Rox says, tugging me

through the door. Inside is a stage in the middle with dozens of seats around it in a circle. The stage is hidden behind big blue curtains, so I can't see what is inside.

"Ten gold for entry. Best hurry, the show starts soon," a gold-skinned man instructs, holding out a tablet. Rox pulls out a thin tablet from his cloak and places it on top of the man's tablet. They both flash before the man nods and steps back to let us in. We make our way through the steps until we find a mostly empty row and sit down. On the end of our row is a little gold-skinned girl with silver hair, with her parents on either side of her. She looks over and waves at me, and I can't help but wave back before looking away.

"What were your questions you wanted to ask?" Rox asks as we wait for the show to start.

"Oh, what powers do all the races have? I know the people of Strixa were gifted with super strength," I say.

"Yes, we are. No other race can beat us in strength, but I could not outrun a man from Noveta. They were gifted with incredible speed," he starts to explain to me. "The Tabre race, like the family at the end of this row, have control over animals. They can speak to them and sing them into a trance. The Illon race can hear for miles, and finally, the Gie race from Giea are who we are about to see. They can control water and breathe under it for a long time."

Drums start going off at the end of Rox's sentence, almost like he planned it, which would be impossible. I turn back to the stage as the curtain rises slowly, revealing massive floating bubbles filled with different colour water. Some have unusual fish swimming around in them, their scales reflecting the bright lights shining down on them so they look pretty and exotic. Music starts to play as the lights move and suddenly go up, shining on two people. A couple stands hand in hand, their dark silver skin gleams as does their long gold hair falling around them. The man is broad shouldered, wearing only tight woven shorts, and the woman has a woven bikini of some kind draped across her body. They both have shimmering blue fabric-like cloaks hanging from their shoulders, which fall onto the floor behind them.

At the same time, they dive right off the top of the stage, each into one of the bubbles of water. The fish surround them like a dance as they swim around, and then they jump out of the bubble and into another one, swimming through the water and spinning around. I'm mesmerized by the dance they do, the way the fish swim around them, and it all just works to make the most amazing thing I have ever seen. Rox wraps his arm around me, and I sink into his side, a tiny part of me aware this is another date without him ever really asking.

It makes me smile.

"This is the best date I've ever been on," I quietly tell Rox. His lips press onto the side of my head, kissing me softly, and for the first time, I realise I'm falling in love with him.

"I never dated before you if I'm being honest. A relationship was never something I was looking for," he tells me. "Now I want to take you on a million dates. Would you be up for that?"

I turn to him, the water dancers completely forgotten, and lean closer, kissing him softly. He kisses me back with just as much tenderness, and I don't know how long we just kiss, but it feels like the start of our forever.

CHAPTER THIRTEEN

"What the fresh new alien hell is this?" I moan as I cover my ears in bed, a loud alarm blasting harshly in my ears as a lovely wake-up call. I barely get a second to adjust to the noise when suddenly I'm thrown out of the bed, and I smack onto the wall, my bedding falling around me and pillows smacking me in the face. I cry out in pain from my shoulder, even as I continue to roll across the floor and try to grab hold of anything to save myself. *What is happening to the ship?*

Slamming into the other side of the room, which damn well hurts, the ship finally stops moving. Pushing the blankets off my legs, I stand up and hold my shoulder as I pull the door open. The blaring alarms make it impossible to hear anything but that noise as I get into the corridor, which is completely empty. Rushing, I jog to the end of the corridor and into the clearing. Everything is smashed to pieces, and it takes me only a second to realise I'm not alone.

In the centre of the room are two men, alien men with deep golden skin and pointy ears coming out of the silver helmet each wears covering his face. Silver metal armour covers his body except for his arms and lower legs, and in his hands are two swords. Kinda swords. They are thin and I think gold, but at the moment, they are dripping with green blood. At his side is a creature that resembles a wolf, but its fur is gold, and its large silver teeth hang from its curled-up lips.

Fear slams into me as I back up and the wolf takes a step forward, its claws digging into the tiles and making an awful noise. *I've never seen a creature like this before.*

"Get her," the man demands, his thick accent reminding me of humans from Ireland. Just about understandable. I scream as I run across the clearing towards the open doors to the cafeteria. I don't know why I didn't turn around and go to my room, but as I run, all I can think about is escaping the wolf.

I don't get far.

The wolf jumps on me, clamping its jaws around

my arm, and I cry out in pain. It lets me go, staying over me as I roll on my back and look up to see it hanging over me, my blood dripping from its long teeth onto my chin.

My fight or flight instinct kicks in, and remembering the training Rox gave me, I curl my fist and punch the wolf in its eye. The wolf howls, giving me enough time to climb to my feet, holding my arm as I stumble backwards. The wolf shakes its head and lets out a long growl that sends shivers through me.

Before I can even think about running, Rox runs past me and throws himself on the wolf, grabbing its neck even as it tries to fight him off. In two moves, Rox snaps the wolf's neck and drops the body to the floor. Straightening up, he pulls two swords out of holders on his back and looks over his shoulder at me.

"Don't move."

Speechless, I can only nod, and Rox looks back at the alien intruder who runs at him. They clash with their swords, light bursting off the metal as they move fluidly around each other. They move so fast, fast enough that I now know for certain Rox was never even trying when we practised fighting the other day. Rox somehow jumps over the intruder's sword and kicks him hard in the face in a backflip. The intruder falls to the floor, and Rox lifts his sword.

"You. Should. Have. Never. Touched. Her!"

With a swing, he stabs the alien in the chest, and I gasp, stumbling until my back hits the wall by the doors to the cafeteria even as warm gold blood coats my skin from this distance. Rox turns to me and runs over, cupping my cheek, but shock holds me silent as I can only see the dead alien on the floor and Rox covered in blood that is not his.

"I fought to get to you. The ship has been attacked and boarded by dozens of Tabres from the planet of Tabrerth. They want the prisoner we have, and I have to make sure they don't get him. I need you to hide until this is over. Ok?" he asks me, and I stare up at him. "I will be back for you. No one is going to touch you. Ever. You're mine."

"Okay," I whisper, tears stinging my eyes. "Are you going to be okay? You won't get hurt, will you?"

"I'm a warrior, and my mate is so fierce she punched a Tabre wolf in the face. I will be fine," he tells me, and I chuckle. I lean up and kiss him softly. Just for a moment. Just because I needed to feel his lips against mine.

Just because I know, when I was about to die...I thought of him. My alien man who stole me from the Earth and took me to the stars.

I break the kiss first as a loud explosion sounds in

the distance, and Rox looks over his shoulder with an angry glint in his eyes when he turns back. "Come on."

Rox hurries me into the cafeteria, past all the overthrown tables to a small room at the back. Using his hand on the pad on the wall, a door swings open to a small storage cupboard with packets of food all over the floor that have fallen from the shelves. "Stay in here until I come for you. Don't open this door for anyone else."

"No one else," I agree, stepping into the storage. Rox looks reluctant to leave as he turns to go, but we both know he needs to help his men and keep whoever is prisoner secured. The door snaps shut before I can see him walk away, leaving me in the darkness of the room as I slide to the floor. My arm stings, and I run my fingers across the bite on my upper arm, feeling the many holes from the wolf's teeth. Thankfully, he only bit me and didn't rip my arm off like he could have done.

At least half an hour passes as I sit in the storage cupboard, and suddenly I hear a woman scream, sounding very close.

"Stay back!" Marnie screams, and I stand up, hearing the fear in her voice. Dammit. I have to open the closet. I search the wall for a gap to open the door and I find a small button. I press it and the door swings open. Marnie is hunched behind a desk, and three Tabre men are walking towards her.

"Marnie, here!" I shout, catching all of their attention. Marnie shoots her head towards me and runs over as fast as she can, with the three Tabre men right behind her, their large legs making the run much faster than she is. She just gets to me as one of them catches her hair, dragging her to the floor as she screams. The bigger of the three walks right up to me and grabs my chin with his beefy gold hand.

"These two will be brilliant breeders. I will enjoy fucking their cunts until they produce a child," he boasts, not looking at me, and I hold in a scream as he roughly tightens his grip on my chin until it really hurts. "She doesn't scream. I like that. Will you scream for me, pretty Earthling?"

"Fuck you," I spit out, and his eyes blaze with anger before he slaps me hard around the face, and I fall to the floor. He picks me up, pulling me against his body.

"Let them go," an unfamiliar voice demands. The Tabre man holding me drops me on the floor like a doll, and I look over to see a man with clear blue skin, shirtless with rippling muscles and strange tattoos covering his ribs on either side. His hair is soft blond in colour, and he is handsome, like most of the alien men are. What planet are the blue aliens from again? And why have I never seen this man on this ship?

"Or what, pretty boy?" the man in front of me coldly asks, his voice dripping with condescension.

The blue guy looks at me, meeting my eyes with his dark blue ones before looking to Marnie, who is now on the floor, passed out. They must have hit her. Anger rises up in me as I meet the blue guy's stare and nod once.

Please kill them.

"You will all die," the blue guy replies.

The Tabre men all laugh, pulling out their swords as a show of power, considering the blue guy has no weapon on him. He literally has nothing but black trousers on, not even any shoes.

"Isn't he the one we came for?" one of the Tabre men asks another one.

"Yes, but the boss only said he wanted him back. Never mentioned anything about the prisoner being alive," another one replies. "Maybe we—" The Tabre man halts mid-sentence as a strange noise fills the room, like something moving superfast. Two more sounds ring out, and suddenly the three Tabre men fall to the ground. Dead. I look up at the blue man, seeing a gun of sorts in his hand.

"Why bother with swords when you have a gun?" he almost jokily asks me, lowering the weapon. "Is your friend alright?" I don't answer him as I stand up and run to Marnie. I turn her over onto her back, seeing a lump growing on the side of her head dotted with blood from a small cut. I feel her pulse and breathe out a sigh of relief that she is alive.

"She is okay. Thank you—" I pause, seeing the blue man is no longer in the room. Well, I guess I can thank whoever he is later. Straightening my injured arm, I try not to pass out from the pain as I grab Marnie's shoulders and pull her to the closet. I have to pause several times, the pain making me breathless, but eventually, I get her into the closet. Using my hand, I press my palm against the pad, and it locks shut with her in there.

"Time to find myself a new hiding place," I mutter, knowing there is no way to lock myself inside with her, because there is no pad inside to lock the door. No, I can find a new space to hide. I rush to the doors of the cafeteria, peeking out and seeing it is empty.

I step out and rush down the corridors to my room. I use my palm to open the door, but it doesn't open, and suddenly there is a loud bang that makes my ears ring. I kneel down, covering my ears from the noise, and I suddenly start to float. Before I can grab anything, a sucking noise infiltrates the room, and I scream into nothing as I am sucked to the end of the corridor and out into cold space.

I want to say I'm brave in my last seconds as I start to freeze, gasping for air, my body shutting down in pure shock. My eyes hurt and sting as I see the edge of the force field around the ship, knowing I will be dead in a second out there and only a minute in here. *It's so, so cold.*

Strangely, I think only of Rox and how I wish we had more time. More time for everything that we could have had.

I think of my sisters, how I wished I hugged them one last time.

Rox, I'm sorry.

Just as I start to black out, I see Rox jumping off the ship and floating right towards me, looking like the saviour I need so desperately. He will be here at the end, and that makes me smile even in these last seconds.

But before he reaches me, everything goes black, and I pass out thinking only of Rox.

CHAPTER FOURTEEN

ROX

I almost lost her.

The same sentence rolls around in my head a dozen times as I hold Darcie in my arms, both of us in the medic bay, in the water that is healing the wounds we both have. Every time I close my eyes, I see Darcie punching a giant Tabre wolf in the face like a warrior, the sheer determination to stay alive the sexiest thing I have ever seen in my life.

The second thing I see is Darcie in space, literally slowly freezing to death, and she just smiled at me like everything was okay.

Like she wasn't fucking dying because I left her alone and I never should have done.

I failed as her mate and nearly lost her, and

fucking hell, I would have killed myself if she had died because of me.

"Rox?" Darcie's melodic voice drifts to me, and I look down at her head resting on my shoulder as she blinks her eyes a few times, waking up in a daze. For the love of Vyuna, Darcie has the most beautiful eyes I have ever seen. I remember the first time I saw her, in a small alleyway. Her determined green eyes met mine, reminding me of the green diamond necklace my mother always wears, and her blonde hair looked like spun gold. Even before I felt the smack of the mating bond telling me she was mine, I admired her.

She helped a boy when she didn't need to, and it hurt her not to help more, I could see that. I believe in my soul Vyuna guided me to Earth to find Darcie, and I swear on my life I will never leave her side.

"How are you feeling?" I ask, tightening my hands around her.

"Are you okay? Is Marnie?" she asks first, thinking of everyone but herself, and it makes me feel blessed.

"I am quite well, and so is Marnie. Marnie claims you saved her life by risking yourself," I comment. "Her mate is in your debt. He told Marnie to run when he was outnumbered by ten Tabres."

"I had some help," she replies to me, her cheeks going red from the compliment. I trace my eyes over her high cheekbones, her big bright eyes and her pouty lips. I could spend hours and hours admiring every inch of this human woman. To me, women are revered and protected, but as for spending time with them, they've never been more than a way to spend a night relieving tension. Darcie though, she makes me never want to leave her side. I want more than a night inside her. I want to be fucking her forever. I have to clear my throat and hope she doesn't feel my hard dick next to her thigh as she keeps talking. "Did they get the prisoner they came for? Did anyone get hurt?"

"No, the prisoner is back behind bars, and they failed. There were two deaths of my men and many injured. We will freeze their bodies for their families to have funerals back home."

"I'm sorry," she whispers, and I feel that she really is as much as I am. When I accepted this mission and chose a hundred soldiers to come with me, I promised to protect them the best I could. When we get back home, I will give the news personally to their parents and mates. I will make sure they have everything they could ever need.

"You saved me...outside," she whispers, placing

her tiny hand on my chest, and I close my eyes, the contact ridiculously pleasurable. "Thank you, Rox."

Looking down, I cup her cheek with my hand, enjoying how she leans into my hand now. "I would jump into a burning tornado for you. Space was nothing."

She chuckles and straightens up. Water drips down her body, emphasizing her curves in the white dress she has on that Zex placed her in for healing. My heart smacks in my chest as she sits fully on my lap, her thighs resting either side of my legs. Her hard nipples rub against my chest as she leans up and kisses me. All self-control flies out of the fucking window as I take her mouth as my own, digging my hands into the soft flesh of her ass. I pull her against my hard cock, enjoying the little moan she lets out into my mouth.

Fucking hell, this woman is going to be the end of me.

"Are you sure?" I break away to ask, to be certain. She smiles and nods once, almost like she is shy, and it makes my dick even harder. I grin, picking her up as I stand and kissing her deeply as I carry her over to the single medic bay.

I'd rather have her in my room, spread out on my bed, but fuck it. Lying Darcie down, I gather the ends of her dress, and she helps me pull it up and off her. I lean back on my knees, looking down at her in front of me.

Fuck, she is perfect. Her curvy body is luxurious, and her breasts are full, a good handful. Between her legs is a small amount of hair, like a landing patch, and I'm desperate to find out how she tastes. I lie on top of her, kissing her once more as her tiny hands undo my trousers. I kiss down her neck, tasting the salty water on her sweet skin. I take notice of how she moans and gasps when I kiss parts of her neck and chest, even as I make my way to her hard nipples. My mate bonds burst to life on my back, I feel them vibrating with the urge to take my mate and mark her as mine as I flick my tongue across her nipples. Her back arches, and little moans leave her lips as I move lower and lower, parting her legs with my hands.

"Rox," she whispers my name like a prayer as I dive between her legs, tasting how sweet she is. Fuck, she tastes perfect. I lick and suck on her clit as I slide one of my fingers into her, feeling how damn tight she is. My dick is painfully hard as I fuck her with my finger, feeling her slowly build up to a release. I slide a second finger inside her, just as she comes on my face and hand, hard and fast, tightening around my fingers.

I pull my fingers out, enjoying her moans as I push my trousers down and grab my cock. I rub it as I stare down at her until she leans up, grabbing my arms and pulling me down to her. Her lips devour mine as I line up at her entrance, her soaking wet cunt teasing me.

"Look at me as I take you as my mate," I demand against her lips. Her bright green eyes lock onto mine as I slowly push inside of her, inch by inch until I'm fully inside her. Her eyes are full of pleasure and desire as we stare at each other. I lean down, taking her lips as mine as I slide out of her and right back in. I thrust in and out of her, enjoying how perfect she feels. This woman was made for me. I know it. I swallow her moans as I own them, enjoying every little noise as she wraps her legs around me, not letting me go.

But fuck, I would never leave. I'd happily die inside of her.

My orgasm starts creeping up on me, but fuck am I coming until she does again. I reach between us, flicking her clit with my finger, and suddenly she cries out as she tightens around my cock, and I come hard. I almost blackout as I come inside her, spilling my seed for what feels like forever in the most intense orgasm of my life. My mating bonds blast across my skin, spreading from my back down my arms and onto her skin, marking her as mine. She doesn't fight the bond as it marks her upper arms and chest with swirls and patterns just like the ones on my back.

"What are these?" she breathlessly asks, looking down at the marks as they settle into her skin. Meeting her eyes, I tell her the fucking fantastic truth.

"It means you're mine, Darcie Lily Jackson. You're my mate."

CHAPTER FIFTEEN

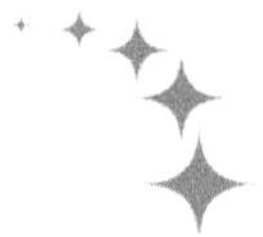

"Someone, not saying *who*, has a certain sex glow about them," Marnie comments, sitting down at my side in the cafeteria, and I try not to choke on my toast. "As well as mating marks on her chest."

"Shhh," I tell her, and she laughs, bumping my shoulder as I look down at the shimmering green markings that match Rox's. They cover my chest and upper arms, and go slightly down my back. It's been three days since Rox and I slept together, well, mated together for the first time, and since then I've hardly left his bedroom. Sex with Rox...well, humans don't do it like aliens do. Aliens apparently are sex gods, and I'm all for spending all my time in bed with Rox until I die of orgasms. Now I might understand why alien groupies are obsessed. But Rox had to leave our bed today to see the captured Tabre prisoner and see if they are talking yet. The ship has been fixed, thanks to alien tech, and it looks brand new even when two parts of the ship were literally destroyed. Rox and his men have no clue how the invaders found the ship; it should not have been that easy, because the ship is cloaked. Rox told me privately that he suspects someone from his home must have betrayed them, given the route away.

"Talk and I will tell you a big secret," she commands, and then she looks nervous for a second, meeting my eyes. "And thank you. Like seriously, thank you for saving me. You risked yourself coming out of hiding for me, and then you gave up your hiding place for me. I don't know how I will ever be able to thank you for that."

"I'm just happy we are both okay now, and yup, I'm having all sorts of alien sexy time with my new mate," I admit, wrapping an arm around her shoulder and hugging her briefly as a big grin lights up her face. "What's your secret then?"

She lowers her voice, just so I can about hear her. "After the attack, healer Zex found out that I am expecting a baby."

A big smile spreads across my lips. I know Marnie wants a baby desperately, and we discussed how they had been trying since the very start, but Marnie had tests done that said she wasn't overly fertile, so it might not happen. "I'm so happy for you."

"Thank you, auntie Darcie," she whispers back and winks at me before going back to her food. I sense Rox way before he even comes into the room, looking furious as he walks in big strides over to me. All I can think about is stripping him naked and climbing him like a monkey until I meet his eyes and know something is wrong.

"I need you to come with me," he asks, holding his hand out.

"What is it?" I question, sliding out of my seat and taking his hand.

"Is everything okay?" Marnie asks.

"Yes and no. Don't worry, Marnie, I'm sure Darcie can catch you up later," Rox tells her, but before I can say bye, we are walking out of the room to the doors and into the corridor before Rox tells me what is going on in a low voice. "One of the captured prisoners was looking for you. He won't talk to anyone but you, and I don't like it, but I want to know why. Will you see him for me? You will be perfectly safe."

"Yes, for you," I answer, and Rox pauses mid-stride and takes my face in his hands, kissing me softly. I can't help but smile back at him as he lets me go, and we make our way across the ship to the elevators. Instead of going in the right one, Rox uses his hand to unlock the left elevator, and we both go inside. Rox presses the lowest button of the row, and the elevator doors snap shut.

"What is so special about the prisoner this mission was about?" I question Rox. I think about the blue alien man who saved me and Marnie, but I haven't seen him on board at all. Rox said the prisoner they came for never escaped his cell even when the door was blasted open. He didn't leave, which makes no sense but it couldn't have been him. Maybe I was just seeing things or something from the stress.

"He killed my oldest brother, the previous crown prince. He is an assassin who was a close friend to my family. Apparently, he killed someone else, someone important to the Tabre race, and they want him dead too. I am taking him back to be put on trial and executed in public for his crimes," he tells me, and I frown at him.

"You never told me your brother was killed. How many siblings do you have?" I question.

"One dead brother who I didn't know that well, another older brother who I hate, and a missing older sister who was stolen as a baby," he tells me. "And you have four sisters, one who was adopted like my currently not-dead brother was."

I chuckle. "Look at us, doing normal things like getting to know each other's family. Finding out which family members you hate. It's almost like dating."

I make him laugh, but it soon dies off as the elevator comes to a stop, and we both step out when the doors open. Rox links his fingers with mine as we walk down a corridor and through the third door down, into a small square room. A Tabre man is strapped to a chair with gold-coloured blood dripping from his face onto his clothes, and his head is dropped down. The room stinks of blood, that metal smell you can almost taste, and it reminds me of when Savannah and I had to kill the last cow on the farm because we couldn't afford to feed and keep it. The smell of all that blood never really leaves you. Strad and another green-skinned man I don't know are at the back of the room, their arms crossed, and Strad's usual playful face is now hard.

"I'm here. What do you want to tell me?" I ask the prisoner, stopping in front of him but not too close. He slowly lifts his head, his long hair dripping into his cold and almost dead looking black eyes. There is something about him that makes me fearful as he laughs.

"You look like her. The girl we took for our king. The sick one," he tells me, and my stomach drops as I shake my head.

"You're lying!" I shout, not believing it.

"Alice, Alice lost in space. But unlike Wonderland, my king will fuck her and breed her until she is dead," he tells me, laughing through his words like a crazy man. "Did you say goodbye? You will never see her again unless you come with me and we both leave this ship with transport. I will take you to her."

Before I can say a word, I look to Rox. Rox doesn't need more than one look in my eyes before he pulls out his sword and swings it straight through the neck of the prisoner, and blood splatters onto my trousers. He almost laughs before the life quickly drains out of him in front of me, and I don't feel anything for him. No guilt, no anger...just pure panic for Alice. Wiping my tears away, I rush out of the room and suck in a breath.

Rox is by my side in seconds, pulling me to his chest and rubbing my back. "It's going to be okay. I have spies on Tabrerth, and when we are home, I will instruct them to find Alice."

"I'm never going to see my sisters again, am I?" I

whisper, trying not to cry anymore. Tears won't get them back. "I chose you, and I will never regret that, but I won't see my sisters again and that hurts. Mum and dad told us to stick together. That family is everything."

"I'm sorry," he tells me, and I know he means it. "If I could fix this, I would. But I won't lose you."

The funny thing is...I couldn't lose him either.

CHAPTER SIXTEEN

"I can't believe you sat through the entire movie," I say as Rox clicks the movie off and looks at me with a smile.

"It was..." He pauses, looking for the right word, and I try not to laugh. "Interesting. Human courting was very strange, but I do see why your mother named you Darcie now."

"Thank you for getting this movie sent over," I tell him, resting my head on his shoulder. "Tell me something about your childhood. What did you like to do as a kid?"

"Climb trees and chase Lulis around the leaves," he tells me, his low voice making me shiver as his thumb rubs circles on my hip.

"What are Lulis?" I question.

"They are small creatures that have big stomachs, tiny heads with big long ears and tiny eyes. They run really fast, and if you startle them, they light up pink and float. I was a mean kid and liked to get them to float and play ball with them," he admits, and I can't help but laugh.

"The poor Lulis!" I say around a laugh.

"My mother used to get so mad and told me I wouldn't like it if someone did that to me," he replies. "And as always, she was right. I stopped after that and started challenging the guards to sword fights. That didn't go down well with my mother either."

I laugh. "So basically you were a pain in the ass as a kid?"

"My mother claimed I was challenging," Rox tells me, and I can just imagine that he was.

"Okay. Tell me about the rest of your family," I ask him. I cover his hand on his knee with my own and link our fingers. My hand's so pale and tiny compared to the light green skin of his large hand, but I do like it. He makes me feel safe.

"My mother was the princess of Strixa, the only heir to the throne, and was due to be mated to the son of a rich family. But my mother liked to escape the castle and go to the beach alone, just to watch the green waters lap against the black sand of the beaches. One day, she came across a man who was washed up on the shore. She called for help, and his life was saved, then the moment he opened his eyes, he told my mother she was his mate. That was my father," he explains to me. "My father was the son of a fishing family whose ship had been attacked by a great monster in the oceans. They mated soon after, and my father challenged my grandfather for the throne, killing him to take it, as he wouldn't back down. He wanted my mother to be mated to the man he chose for her, even if she didn't love him and he wasn't her fated mate."

"Was the other family mad?" I ask.

"Incredibly so. But the son mated eventually, and they had a baby boy just before the dragons came. They were both killed, and my mother adopted the baby boy," he tells me. "Due to the threat we grew up in, we were each separated from each other growing up. I was the lucky one who they chose to stay with them. My other brothers were sent to castles and brought up with nannies. Unfortunately, they both became bitter and cold towards the world."

"You told me your oldest brother was killed, how did that happen?" I ask.

"Someone he grew up with betrayed him. We might never know why, but I will get him justice even if I wasn't a good friend to my brother like I should have been," he honestly tells me. "I wrapped up my entire world in battles and becoming a feared warrior. Nothing else mattered to me until I stopped on Earth and saw a woman with haunting green eyes in an alleyway."

"Oh yeah, what did you like about her?" I teasingly ask, climbing onto his lap and wrapping my arms around his neck. His silver eyes find mine, and every second I spend with him, I get the sense I know him so much more. I could spend forever in his arms, just being with him, learning everything about my mate.

"Her determination. It radiated off her, and she had this amazing ass." He grabs my ass, pulling me against his body. "It took everything in me to walk away."

"I always thought The Mates Lottery was a big joke. That it wasn't real and it only served to find human women for alien douche-bags, but I was wrong," I admit, biting down on my lip. "I'm so happy I won you."

"Technically we won each other," he comments, his husky voice doing wonders for me.

"Oh yeah?" I ask, moving closer so our lips are

inches away from each other. "Well, as winners, we should enjoy our prizes."

"I plan to," he grumbles before kissing me, devouring my lips like a man on a mission. And I'm happily on board.

"WATCHING them fight is a total turn on," Marnie whispers to me as her mate, Xemak, and Rox fight in the middle of the clearing. They aren't using weapons, just their fists, and they are both topless and sweaty.

Marnie is not wrong.

Rox grabs Xemak by the waist and flips him over his shoulder, sending him flying backwards into the wall, and he lands with a smack. Now normal people would say ouch or groan, but Xemak and Rox laugh as Rox jogs over and offers him his hand to pull him up.

"I'm going to steal Xemak for some quiet time... you know, in my bed," Marnie tells me before running over and jumping into Xemak's arms. He carries her out of the training room, and Rox laughs as he walks over to me.

"Have I ever told you you're a great fighter?" I say

as he stops in front of me, and I run my eyes over his sweaty chest. "Like really sexy good fighter?"

"And you're beautiful. Is there a reason for your very welcome presence this early in the morning?" he asks before leaning down and kissing me softly.

"Yes, I made you breakfast... Okay, I stole us breakfast from the kitchens," I admit, holding up the bag at my side. "I thought we could sit somewhere and eat."

"Sounds perfect. Why don't you make your way to my room while I quickly shower?" he asks, and I grin, kissing his cheek before skipping out of the room. The common area is super busy today, full of men on the tablets, and I peek over someone's shoulder to see they are all watching the same show. It looks like a competition between all the races, and they are riding strange horses through a forest. I may be in space, but aliens love their shows just as much as humans do. I happily head for Rox's rooms, letting myself in and wondering for the first time if I'm actually living with him now. We never actually discussed that I've moved in, but I sleep here every night and I haven't been back to my room in a long time. I set up some pillows by the window, overlooking a bright blue planet that we are passing by. By the time I've set up all the food, Rox comes into the room in a white shirt and tight black trousers. A smile doesn't leave his lips as he walks over and sits next to me, stretching his long legs out and picking up some of the red fruits. They look like strawberries, but they aren't.

And I don't have a clue what their real name actually is.

"What planet is that?" I ask, pointing out the window at the blue planet that looks cold. Very cold.

"Giea. The people live underwater, mostly, and the top is all frozen, with occasional hot spots where they grow food and harvest the clean water," he explains to me. "They used to have much darker skin when the planet wasn't all frozen over. But that was thousands of years ago, and all the time under the ice has turned their skin a strange silver colour like you saw. We are currently hidden from their scanners as we are at war."

"I wonder why you are green, and everyone in the universe has such vivid colours," I ponder.

"I can answer that one," he tells me before taking a deep bite of his toast. "The pigments in the water had a deep effect on our appearance. Many of our scientists have researched this in great detail."

"The more I hear of Strixa, the more I can't wait

to see it," I tell him, and he smiles as he hands me a green-coloured fruit that reminds me of a banana.

"I can't wait to show you home too," he replies, and we both start eating in a comfortable silence, watching a planet go by like it's a totally normal thing.

For us, it kinda is, and I wouldn't have it any other way.

CHAPTER SEVENTEEN

Closing my eyes, I try not to look down, knowing I will freak out and be a total coward if I do. Over my dead body am I looking like a coward in front of all these alien men who are watching. The damn green bastards have bets on me not doing this, I just know it. Marnie can't do the agility course, so it's down to me to prove women aren't silly wallflowers on this ship.

"Wolf puncher! Wolf puncher!" Strad, Zex, Marnie and all the guys shout. Rox looks close to laughing as I glare at them. That name is never going to go away.

Pushing out a calming breath to steel myself, I jump off the ledge and swallow a scream as I free-fall straight down and crash into the warm water below. I swim to the bottom, pulling my eyes open and seeing the yellow flag waiting for me. Diving further down, I stretch my hand out and grab the flag before swimming to the surface. I gasp for air when I break the surface and hold up the flag in the air victoriously. Marnie cheers and claps, Rox laughs and the rest of the bastards grumble as they hand their money over to each other.

I swim to the edge, and Rox leans down, picking me up out of the water, plastering me to his chest. I hook my legs around his waist and grin. "Told you I could do it."

"You can do anything you put your mind to, my mate," he whispers and kisses me. I sink my hands into his hair, forgetting where we are, only focusing on how he feels against me. Only caring about Rox.

"Whoa! My eyes!" Marnie dramatically protests, and I laugh, breaking away and hiding my head in Rox's shoulder.

"Everyone resume training. I will be back soon," Rox shouts to the men and carries me away.

"I can walk, you know," I tell him, arching an eyebrow as I lean back. When he smiles back at me, his dimples stretch his beautiful face.

"I am aware. I do need to speak to you about something," he tells me quite seriously but never puts me down until we are back in his room. He puts me down on the bed, kneeling between my legs and pulling out a small purple vial from his pocket.

"What is that?" I ask, leaning up on my elbows.

"Birth control. I want children with you, Darcie. I want your belly filled with our babies, but I won't push you into this decision. You mean more to me, and it is your body, Darcie," he tells me, and tears fill my eyes as my heart beats fast.

"Rox...dammit. You are so sweet, and I'm never going to be able not to love you, am I?" I question. He laughs, leaning down and kissing me. I roll us over, well, he lets me, and I rest on top of him. I take the vial from his hand and look at it for a long time, just thinking over everything.

Do I want kids?

I know if I were asked that a year ago, I would have said, *yes but in the future, with the right guy.* Honestly, I've always wanted a child, and it has crossed my mind several times since mating with Rox that a child would be a blessing for us.

I smile at Rox and throw the vial off the bed. His eyebrows rise as I run my hands up his muscular chest.

"I choose you, and I want a future. I want a baby, a family with you," I admit, biting down on my lip. "I love you, and I feel we were always looking for each other. You challenge me, you protect me and don't care that I'm a pain in the ass most of the time. I know you wouldn't ever leave me, and I would never go anywhere without you. Rox...I never for a second thought this could work when we met. I just wanted to kill you, if I'm being honest...but now I could not imagine living without you at my side. Is that okay that I want a baby with you? I want to see what our children would be like and raise them together."

"Is that okay?" he repeats my question with wonder in his eyes. Rox runs his hands through my hair, making me shiver, and pulls me down to him, our lips inches away from each other. "It's perfect. You are perfect for me, Darcie. Now I'm going to fuck you until you're carrying my baby in that sweet belly of yours, and I am never leaving your side. All the stars in the universe couldn't keep you from me."

His lips devour mine without a second to pause, and his large hands literally rip my top off me. Holy heckballs, it's the sexiest thing I've ever seen. Flipping us over on the bed, Rox holds my jaw as he kisses down my chest and between my breasts, going lower with every single teasing kiss.

Like the expert he is, he sinks between my legs, licking and sucking on my clit until I'm so close to the edge of an orgasm that I don't recognise the sounds coming out of my mouth. Before I can come, Rox stops and flips me over on the bed, pulling my hips up and kneeling behind me. He quickly slides his thick cock into me, filling me to the brim before pulling out and slamming harder the next time. I moan, the new position hitting just the right spot with every thrust. Rox wraps my hair around his hand, pulling my head back and sucking on my neck as he thrusts in and out of me.

"Come on my cock," he commands, his husky voice sending me spiralling into an orgasm. I moan I tip over the edge, and he thrusts faster, making my orgasm last longer until he lets my hair go and grabs my hips, holding me in place as he comes hard. I feel his hot come filling me up as he lets out a sensual groan before pulling out of me and lying down as I fall onto the bed.

Breathlessly I rest on Rox's chest, and he kisses the top of my head, holding me so close to his side.

"I have something I have been meaning to give to you," he tells me, climbing to his feet and walking naked across his rooms. I watch his ass the entire way, admiring how tight and damn sexy he is. His mating marks cover his back, matching mine that shine slightly against my skin when we have sex and afterwards fade normally. I love the markings; they mean so much more than a simple ring to announce a couple marrying or mating on Earth. Rox comes back to the bed with a long silver box, and I take it from him. I push the box open, and inside is a stunning diamond bracelet. Pink diamonds line the silver bracelet, the diamonds so large you can see all the way through them.

"This was my mother's. She gave it to me many years ago and said it was a gift to my mate when I find her, and she demanded I take it with me wherever I went, even when I was not looking for a mate," he tells me, picking the bracelet up from the box, and I lift my arm for him to clip it on. The bracelet almost fits perfectly, and it's so beautiful.

"I will have to thank her," I say with a soft smile. "It reminds me, I have a necklace my mum and dad left to me in my will. It will actually match this one, it's a pink diamond, but the chain is broken. Can we have it fixed when we are home?"

"You have no idea how much I love hearing you call my planet home," he replies, linking our fingers together. "And yes. I will have it fixed for you. May I ask a personal question?"

"You can ask me anything," I tell him, and he smiles.

"How did your parents die?" he asks.

I look down, the diamonds of the bracelet catching my eye. "Where we live, there is heavy marshland a good ten miles away, and one of the cows broke the fence that protected them from the marsh. My parents and we kids went into the marsh to save them. We needed them for milk to sell and food when we had them butchered. We had nearly all of them out when the marsh gave in with my parents above it, and they drowned."

"Darcie, I'm sorry," he tells me, pulling me into his arms and holding me so tightly.

"I didn't see it happen, but Isabelle did. She always felt guilty for not doing something, but she couldn't have saved them. All that would have happened was that she would have died with them," I tell him. "Some nights she would have nightmares, wake up screaming. All of us would pile into the bed with her and just be there so she could sleep. So she knew she wasn't alone."

"Your family sounds very close," he tells me and kisses my head. "I feel guilty I have taken you from them and that I will never give you back," Rox says, caressing my thigh.

"Don't," I whisper, "because even though I miss them, I do not want to go back. I wasn't living before, just surviving, and now I have everything I was searching for."

"You have a way with words, Darcie," he tells me, pushing me back onto the bed and leaning down over me as I grin, always up for a distraction at the hands of Rox. "And now I'm going to show you *my* special talent."

"What is that—" I gasp as he dives between my lips and shows me that his talent is special indeed.

CHAPTER EIGHTEEN

"You have such a big bump now," I tell Marnie as she waddles beside me to the dining room. My cute and six-month pregnant friend just glares at me, and I quickly think of something to divert her attention. "They have those maple pancakes you like in today. I saw them this morning."

"Oh, I do like those." She nods. "But you're a bitch still and lucky I love ya."

I laugh as we get into the cafeteria. I'm only two steps in when an alarm goes off, not the same as the warning one but a low buzzing. Strad jogs over to us, stuffing a pancake into his mouth on the way.

"What does that mean?" I ask Marnie, but Strad answers as he gets to us.

"It's a ship docking alarm," Strad comments. "And I believe you might want to see who is here, Miss Darcie."

"Well, as long as nothing is on fire, I'm eating," Marnie comments as she walks around him and through the tables. "Good luck!"

"Come on," Strad suggests, picking up someone's uneaten toast and shoving it into his mouth as he walks out the room with me.

"Any girl back home lucky enough to have the pleasure of sharing meals with you, Strad?" I ask as we head to the elevator. Strad laughs as he pushes the button and shakes his head.

"None that can handle my sexy charm," he counters, winking at me. I chuckle as the elevator opens, and we both step inside. "I've heard you have sisters. Any single?"

Sadness sinks in my chest as Strad presses the button for the second lowest floor of the ship, somewhere I haven't been before. "They are lost in space. I couldn't find them for you if I tried."

Strad doesn't reply, and I'm thankful he doesn't as the elevator goes down, and then the doors open. This room is huge, like a big open warehouse with massive doors at the one side, and a small ship is inside, right in front of them. Rox with five of his guards and Zex wait in a line in front of the ship, and Rox looks back. He holds his hand out for me, and I rush over, stepping to his side as I take his hand.

"This ship is from Idillon," Rox tells me as a walkway slides out of the black ship to the ground, and a door slides open. I expect to see the two purple-skinned, almost naked—bar a cloth around their junk—alien men but not the woman in the middle of them.

"Savannah!" I cry out, wanting to run to her, but Rox holds me close to his side.

"Darcie...," she whispers in shock, but I hear her.

"It's a trade," Zex whispers to me from my other side. "You can't go to her yet, but she looks well to me. They clearly have cared for her."

"Okay. Thank you so much, Rox. I can't believe you did this for me," I say, keeping my eyes on Savannah the whole time as they walk her down the pathway and stop a good distance away, holding onto her upper arms the entire time.

"I would do anything for you. I wish I could find all your sisters, but so far, only Savannah was easily found," he quietly tells me.

The purple dudes bow their heads, and I see

everyone but Rox do the same thing. When I go to do it, Rox shakes his head at me.

"Royals never bow," he softly instructs me, "Princess Darcie."

"Oh shit, right." I nod. One of the purple dudes coughs out a laugh as he straightens.

"We have the female you requested. Do you have the water we requested in return?"

"All this is for you." Rox points at the dozens of barrels on the one side of the room. "Would you like my men to help you carry the water on board?"

"It would be appreciated," the man states, bowing his head once more. "The female is wild, I must inform you. None of our men could mate with her due to her character."

"And she bites," the other man bitterly adds in, and I try not to laugh.

"If you don't let me go, you purple-headed asshole, I'm going to bite you *again*! And you are going to cry *again*!" Savannah shouts, pulling her arms from the men and running to me. I open my arms as she crashes into me, and I squeeze her so tight as I try not to cry, but I fail quickly.

"I missed you," she whispers to me, crying just like me. "Are you okay? Do we need to jump ship?"

"I'm happy, Sav. I'm so happy," I tell her, holding her as tightly as I can. "I can't believe you're here."

"Some prince set up a trade for me. Which one of these guys do I need to thank?"

"My mate and the man I love. Rox," I tell her as she lets me go, and Rox steps to my side, wrapping his arm around my waist. His other hand, he stretches out for her. Sav's eyebrows couldn't go higher as she stares at us both.

"Holy shit, my sister is in love," she whispers. "I'm speechless."

"First time for everything," I chuckle, and she joyfully laughs as she shakes Rox's hand.

"Thank you for trading me and for apparently winning my sister's heart. I expected her to have killed you and everyone on board by now," she says...only kinda joking. Rox laughs as he lets her hand go.

"Death threats were an early part of our courting," he tells her, and I playfully whack his chest with my hand. He laughs and kisses the top of my head, letting me go. "I must stay and talk with the Illons before they leave. I'm sure you wish to spend time with your sister alone."

"I do, thank you," I say and lean up, kissing him softly before he leaves us. Savannah hooks her arm in mine as we walk to the elevator, and I can't stop looking her way, and it seems the same for her.

"Tell me what happened at the farm after I managed to knock myself out," I ask her as I place my hand on the pad, and it scans it before beeping and opening up. I press the button to go up, and the doors slide shut.

"I saw that. It would have been funny under any other circumstances," she jokes, and her voice drifts off as the elevator goes up. "We spent the night in the farm, and in the morning the cars turned up. It was the last time I saw any of our sisters."

I keep the conversation light as we walk through the ship, and most of the guys stop to stare at the new human female on board. Sav doesn't seem to notice at all.

"Whoa, this is a nice room. But why all the black stuff?" Sav asks, sitting on the couch and stretching her legs out.

"Rox loves the colour. I actually made him a black fabric notebook from my old clothes and paper that he carries around in training. It took hours to make," I say with a small smile as I sit next to her. I snuggle up to her side, resting my head on her shoulder. "I found out news about Alice."

Sav moves quickly, looking me in the eye as she

straightens. I get it, I've always felt overprotective of Alice because there was always a risk she would be gone in seconds if her illness took her. "Where is she?"

I quickly explain everything that happened with the prisoner, and by the end, Sav looks as worried as I feel.

"I will stay here until we get to the planet, and then I'm going to find her," Sav announces. "I can't let her die on some planet as a prisoner."

"I wish I could come with you, but I won't leave Rox," I admit to her, and her expression softens.

"You really love him. How did that happen?" she asks, taking my hand and squeezing it tightly.

I look out the glass window, at the spiralling space as we fly through it. "Mum and dad were in love. That true love you envied every time you saw it because it's so rare. I honestly believed I would never find that; I never saw that potential for love in anyone else I met until Rox stormed into my life. There was just something about him, and slowly my heart made sure I knew it was love. I don't believe in fate or that things are meant to be. I just believe if you want to be with someone that badly, you do everything you can for the rest of your life to make it work. And for me? That someone is Rox."

"I'm so happy for you. And a little jealous," she tells me, and I grin.

"Good news! This ship is full of single sexy alien men," I say, and she laughs. I hug her one more time, and I honestly never want to let go.

CHAPTER NINETEEN

"The cat went to-to the map to find his h-a-t," Mick sounds out the sentence, and I clap my hands with Marnie, who has taken Mick as a kind of teacher to him. Mick looks so proud and like he is nearly a different kid now he is eating right. His dusty brown hair is all shiny, his cheekbones have filled out, and he is the cutest little kid now.

"Very good, Mick. You're doing brilliantly," Marnie tells him, and he beams. Rox is sure one of the many children-less families on Strixa will jump at the chance to adopt him when we land at home in less than a month. I'm so happy for Mick, and I hope the new family will let me keep in contact with him as he grows up. I mess up his hair as I stand up, and he playfully shoves me away as I look at Marnie.

"I have a lunch date, but I want to check on Sav on the way. See you later?" I ask, and she shrugs.

"I don't know how I could escape you on this tiny ship," she replies and winks, making Mick laugh. I chuckle as I leave Marnie's rooms and head past my own to the medical bay. The door is open, and I pop in, seeing Sav sitting at a desk, looking into a microscope. Her clothes match mine, and her long hair is up in a high ponytail, falling down her back and shoulders as she looks down.

"Healer Savannah, can I have a moment of your time?" I ask, teasing her, and she shoots up, turning to face me as she swings her chair around.

"Hey, sis. What you up to today?" she asks.

"I have a lunch date with a special someone," I tell her, leaning against the water pods. This room will always remind me of mating with Rox, and the thought makes my cheeks start to burn a little bit.

"Lucky you. I stay in here to avoid the men on this ship," she mutters, and I try not to chuckle but fail. "If I get one more weird-ass gift, I'm going to jump into space."

"Aww, they just think you're beautiful," I tell her.

"No, they think I'm fertile, which is why they keep leaving poems that talk of—" She pauses.

"Either way, they see me as a baby machine, and that isn't hot."

I turn around as Sav keeps talking, sensing that he is nearby just as he walks past and stops, turning towards me. I run my eyes over Rox's tight white shirt with green clips at the side and tight black trousers that I love ripping off him. His black hair is styled to the side of his forehead, a few locks falling astray that I want to gently brush aside with my fingertips. His lips tilt up when he sees me, so do mine, and instantly my heart starts to pound away in my chest.

Looking at Rox is like seeing my home. The home I've always searched for. The one place I will always feel safe in this galaxy.

"Ready for our date?" Rox asks, offering me his hand. I don't hesitate as I take it, and he tugs me to him, leaning down and kissing me deeply.

"This is a medical bay, not a high school, guys," Sav says, reminding us she is still here, and I chuckle as I break away from the kiss.

"Always a pleasure to see you, Savannah. How are you enjoying the ship?" Rox asks her as I tuck myself into his side.

"It's very interesting. How is the search for Chloe going?" she counters.

Rox sighs. "We know Alice is on the planet Tabrerth, and we are waiting for my spy to tell us if she is safe. Chloe is still an unknown. She was due to travel to the planet Giea to meet her mate, but we cannot get in touch with the ship taking her. The Giea high council have a serious issue with space pirates taking their ships due to the high amount of weapons on board. The Giea race do make most of the weapons for the galaxy, and therefore the pirates have a vested interest in their ships."

"You're suggesting Chloe has been stolen by space pirates?" I ask.

"I cannot tell you the correct answer to that for certain, but I will do everything in my power to find out and save your sisters, Darcie," he softly tells me.

"Thank you for everything you have done so far," Sav tells him before I can. "Now go and make my sister happy with a no doubt panty-dropping date."

Rox can only laugh at her statement as my cheeks burn.

"Bye, Sav," I say around a chuckle as I drag Rox from the room before Sav can embarrass me anymore. I'm so happy to have my sister back, but if she tells Rox one more story of when I did silly stuff and deadly embarrassing stuff, I'm going to chuck her back into space.

"Where are you taking me today then?" I ask, resting my head on his massive arm.

"Home. In a sense," he cryptically tells me, and I give him a surprised look. We head right past his rooms and to the elevator that I think leads to the engine room, but I've never found out. Rox opens the elevator, and we head inside. There are two buttons and another scanner inside that Rox has to use before the doors will close, and then the elevator goes up. When it opens, I'm not surprised to see the engine room with a single chair in front of a giant semi-circle raised touchpad console with a range of buttons at the top. The wall in front is all glass in the shape of a huge triangle, with a point at the top and slanting cathedral-like ceilings, and in the distance is a planet I have only seen in picture books.

"Is that our home planet?" I ask, walking around the empty seat and console to the front of the glass, which showcases a planet that has a circle of falling diamonds surrounding it. The diamonds shine, reflecting the sun in the distance, and they move in waves around the very green planet inside. Green seas and darker green land can be seen through the falling diamonds surrounding it. It looks like a green jewel in a sea of stars. Rox steps up behind me and lifts his hands over my shoulders to show me my mum's necklace in his hands, on a new silver chain.

Tears fill my eyes as I stare at the necklace.

"For the first time you see our home, I thought a little token of your old home would be special. I do hope you will forgive me for searching your room for the necklace," he asks me.

"Rox, thank you so much," I whisper, lifting up my hair for him. The necklace rests in the middle of my chest as Rox does up the clasp, and I let my hair fall. I turn around and lean up, kissing him deeply. He cups the back of my head as I work on his belt, undoing the clasp and pulling his hard cock out into my hand. Softly brushing my lips against his, I lean back and fall to my knees.

I've never done this with anyone before. I never thought the idea of submitting to a guy sexy until now. Until Rox.

I lean forward and wrap my lips around the thick tip of Rox's cock, and he groans, sinking his hands into my hair. I slowly take as much of him as I can into my mouth before moving. Rox slowly guides me, showing me how he likes it, and I dig my hands into his thighs. After a few minutes, Rox stops me and pushes me down onto the floor. I help him take my clothes off before he easily slides inside me, filling me to my core.

"I love you. You are mine," he growls against my lips as he fills me again and again, making it impossible to think of anything else.

"I love you too," I gasp just as I crash into an orgasm, and Rox swallows my cries like they belong to him.

And they do. Just like me. I only belong to my alien prince.

CHAPTER TWENTY

"I can't wait to be off this ship and dig my feet into the grass. By the way, the grass here is always cold even when the weather is warm. How weird is that?" Marnie asks me, standing at my side as we both stare out the window at the main city of Strixa. The city is gigantic, full of spiralling green towers that are covered in moss and trees dotted everywhere that almost look like they are eating the tower buildings. This place looks like something out of a fantasy book that Alice would read, and I really wish she were here to see this place.

"What is the city called again?" Savannah asks me from my other side.

"Satita, the first city of green light," I say, remembering what Rox told me about this place. There are five main cities on Strixa but thousands of villages hidden in the massive rainforests. Rox explained that the ocean used to be blue, but since the dragons' blood, it is now green, and nothing they have done has changed the colour back. "The city is just stunning."

"Darcie," Rox calls me over. I say goodbye to Marnie and Sav, knowing they will be leaving the ship later than we will, and head over to my mate who waits in the middle of the main area. He looks amazing in clothes I've never seen him in before. Almost like robes, the deep green material wraps around his chest with several glittering diamond badges clipped on. On his head is a small crown littered with green diamonds that catch the light. Two swords, his swords, are clipped to his sides and reach just above the ground at their tips. I feel very underdressed in my usual stretchy material clothes, and my blonde hair is super wavy today from sleeping with it in a plait. Rox doesn't seem to care when I step in front of him, and he leans down, kissing me softly. "We will be landing soon, and I need you at my side to introduce to my family. Remember, royals do not bow, and you are my mate. My princess."

"That's a title I will never be used to. Or seeing

you with a crown," I admit, and he grins, wrapping his arms around me as the ship wobbles a little and goes still.

"Well, the parade waiting to see the new princess outside is going to freak you out," he tells me, and I widen my eyes. "Don't worry. I will never leave your side."

I don't say a word as I take Rox's hand, and with our five guards, including Strad, surrounding us, we head to the elevator. It's crowded inside, and a nervous silence surrounds us, or it just might be me feeling that way as every second seems to drag on. I'm sure I look like a nervous wreck as the elevator opens up to the bottom floor of the ship where the back part is now open, and a single pathway extends down to stone pavement outside. Cheers fill my ears and the space around us as we walk to the pathway, and for the first time, I get a good look at the outside of the ship. Thousands and thousands of alien people, mostly green-skinned, crowd the area. It's also the first time I get a real good look at the women. They are stunning with dark black hair, which most wear in two braids with several gold or silver ring clips breaking up their hair. They don't wear tops, just thin fabric that falls to their waists and into long skirts. They are beautiful.

"Now I'm not sure what to be more freaked out about: meeting your parents or the whole city, it seems," I mutter to Rox, and he leans down, kissing the side of my head, and the crowd cheers even louder. Slowly a floating boat-like ship flies over the crowd and lands at the clearing. Rox walks us right up to it, our guards moving around us like a bubble. Two of the guards climb into the ship first, and Rox lifts me by my waist, placing me on the boat ship. I quickly sit down as he climbs on next. A force field covers the boat ship as soon as the last guard boards, and then it takes off, heading for the massive spiral towers in the middle of the city, surrounded by a thick forest of trees that look nothing like the trees from home. These trees are made of swirling bark and leaves the size of TVs that wrap around the branches that shoot in lots of directions until they find another tree. The further we travel into the city, the trees get closer to the pathways and create bridges over us that people are walking on, and the people are throwing orange-coloured petals into the air, filling the space. It doesn't take long for us to start travelling up and towards an archway that leads to a big square clearing where a line of ten green-skinned aliens wait in black armour with a green sash of shimmering fabric hung over their chest with different badge-like pins attached.

The biggest guard, right in the middle, walks over to the boat ship as it lands us in the clearing. The force field disappears like it was never there, and two of the guards climb out first before Rox gets out and holds his hands out for me. I jump down with his help, and he wraps his arm around my waist as we walk to the big alien man with light grey hair and a stern expression.

The man bows low as soon as we are close, and Rox comes to a stop with me at his side.

"Welcome home, your majesty. It is an honour to meet your new mate," the man says, rising back up and nodding at me when I smile his way. "Your parents and brother are waiting in the throne room, sir and madam."

"Whoa, it's Darcie. Please don't call me madam again. It basically means old lady on Earth," I tell him, and he pales.

"I am sorry for the—"

"Oh, I didn't mean to be bossy!" I interrupt, and Rox laughs, breaking the tension.

"My beautiful mate is the definition of bossy," he says, his eyes twinkling with mischief. I love when

Rox is playful, it just makes my heart beat that bit faster.

"Am not," I counter, raising an eyebrow.

"Lead on, Kalkols," Rox replies around a laugh, and poor Kalkols bows his head. Rox lowers his voice as we walk behind Kalkols through the waiting line of other guards. "Kalkols is the royal head guard of Satita. When I was a child, he saved my life when I attempted to try and fly like the birds off the top of the castle."

Kalkols looks back, a smile on his lips that does not match his stern appearance. "After the fall, I became Rox's personal trainer and guard. He became a fine warrior, and I am proud to have his respect."

"I am proud to have you as my friend, Kal," Rox replies, and there is a smirk on Kal's face as he turns back. They don't speak anymore as we get inside the main part of the castle, and it's beautiful...like nothing I could have ever imagined. Green pools of water stream around pillars that are covered in red ivy that snakes up to the verandas. Large rocks cascade around the stream, and dozens of flowers cover the space, flowers like I've never seen before. The bright colours of the place, mixed with the clearly old feeling of the building makes this place look like a forgotten wonder I only saw in books at school.

"How has it been since I left?" Rox quietly asks when we get around a corner and turn into a silent corridor.

"The same as usual, sir," Kal replies tightly, and the way Rox's jaw pulses suggests he isn't happy with that news. "I just received word the prisoner from your ship is being transported over. The king has requested to see the prisoner immediately."

"We will be staying for that," Rox replies, his grip tightening on my hand.

"I would suggest as much, sir," Kal replies when we get to glass doors. Two guards stand in front of them, and they both bow before stepping to the side and pulling the doors open. The throne room is incredible.

Just breathtaking.

Hundreds of giant flowers grow from the ground, reaching up and filling the ceiling and every corner of the room, green grass that looks so alive smothers the ground, and two streams of sparkling green water make their way through the room in strange patterns. On the walls, almost hidden between the flowers, I spot massive paintings of royals, the crowns being mostly the only bit of clothing they wear. I duck my head and focus on the back of the room where the flowers curl around a massive tree. In the tree are two thrones with incredible drawings carved into the wood, and the seats are not empty.

A man that could be a twin of Rox sits in one of the seats, dressed in green robes with a massive amount of badges clipped onto it, making it look heavy. The crown on his head is made of glowing green roots that hold three palm-sized light green crystals in the middle, reflecting the glowing light from the roots. He has no hair, his head is completely shaved, and there is a long cut along the one side of his scalp. His eyes meet mine, and even though he seems a little scary, I don't get the impression he is a bad man. The woman at his side stands up, holding her feminine hands tightly together. Her green skin is lighter than her mate's, and her hair is like a black wave falling down her back. Light green robes cover most of her skin, unlike a lot of the alien women I've seen here, and gold bands wrap around her arms all the way to where her shoulder meets her arm. Her crown is just like her husband's, just a little smaller.

When I meet her eyes, I just see Rox. She has the same eyes as him, and everything about her screams kindness.

Rox walks us both up to the throne, and even

when my legs feel like jelly, I keep my head high and smile as much as I can. The king slowly stands up and stares at Rox.

"Welcome home, my son. I cannot explain my delight at hearing you have taken a mate," he says, and it's like the tension just leaves the room as the king embraces his son. A second later, I'm crushed by the queen, who hugs me so tightly.

"My name is Astrid, Rox's mother and queen. In that order." She winks at me, holding onto my shoulders. "I cannot contain my excitement. I hope you can forgive me."

"Hugs are always welcome where I come from. My mum taught me that," I tell her, and she smiles even bigger, which I thought was impossible. "My name is Darcie."

"Such a lovely name." The king turns to me and offers me his hand. I take it, and he kisses the back of my hand. "You may call me Kutod, and welcome to our family. I have waited many years to hear my son has mated."

"Have you given up hope on me then, father?" a new voice taunts, and Rox moves closer to my side as a man steps out from behind the tree before sitting on the side of the throne seat. He doesn't look like Rox or his parents, but I quickly gather this is the adopted brother I've heard about. I look up at Rox, seeing how tense he suddenly is and how he stares down at his brother whose eyes stay fixed on me.

"Don't be a fool, Croveik," Rox growls, stepping in front of me, and his mother moves to my other side.

"Fool, me?" he teases, and I can't see him, but I imagine he has a smile on his face. Astrid looks nothing but sorry, and I peek around Rox to see Kutod has gone back to his throne, his hands crossed on his lap. "A cunt won't make me fight you, brother. Do not worry yourself, that law has no interest to me."

Rox is across the room in seconds, holding his brother by the neck against the throne. Rox has the strength, even if Croveik is about the same height as him. Croveik doesn't fight him back, he just laughs like this is the funniest thing he has ever seen.

"Watch your mouth, or I will fucking break it," Rox growls, slamming his brother's head into the throne to dig the words in. "Look at her, touch her or say one fucking word against Darcie that I don't like, and I will kill you. Do. You. Understand?"

Croveik just laughs, and Rox doesn't drop him until he nods. Croveik falls in a heap onto the floor as Rox leaves him and walks to me, wrapping his arm around my waist, and I lean into him, hoping to comfort him somewhat. Astrid has her hand on Kutod's arm, and she looks distressed, but Kutod doesn't seem remotely bothered by his sons fighting. The doors open behind us, and I turn back to see Strad and another guard escorting an alien man in handcuffs with blue skin and a smirk on his face as he sees me.

Rox looks between us, picking up on something, and I don't know what to say as Strad pushes the man to his knees in front of Kutod.

"Xair'uil from the planet Noveta, do you plead guilty to the crime of high treason and murder of our crown prince?" Kutod coldly asks. The room goes silent as we wait on the answer Xair'uil might give, and guilt fills my chest. I need to tell Rox that he saved me when he didn't need to. He risked escaping the ship to save Marnie and me.

"I did not kill the prince. He was my friend, and I found his body. I was framed for the murder, and I had no choice but to run away. I grew up with Prince Igor from when I was ten, as well you all know, why would I kill him?"

"It was your weapon that killed him," Rox snaps. "And you didn't just run. You killed ten of our guards on your way out and stole Igor's ship."

"I *did* steal the ship and knock out *one* guard. I did *not* do the rest," Xair'uil claims, and while everyone in the room looks at him like he is guilty...I think I believe him. A bad man would not have saved me and Marnie in that room, they would have just left us. He could have taken me or Marnie as hostage, but he didn't. He cared that we were okay.

"Your lies will not save you this time, Xair'uil. I find you guilty of high treason and the murder of the crown prince of Strixa," the king demands.

"No!" I shout, a little too loud as it echoes around the room. I gulp as they all stare at me, and I look up at Rox.

"When the ship was attacked, he saved me. I told you someone saved me in the cafeteria and killed all those Tabre men. It was him, and he made sure we were okay before leaving and getting caught. He saved me. That has to count for something, right?"

Rox is silent as he looks between me and Xair'uil, and I swear I don't feel like I breathe the entire time.

"Is this correct?" Rox asks Xair'uil.

"I may not have liked your posh asshole self as a kid, but I would never let a woman die if I could stop it," he firmly tells Rox. "And who do you think told the Tabre where your ship was? And why did my cell open on its own? One prince is a liar here."

"Thank you for saving my life and Marnie's," I tell Xair'uil when no one speaks for a long time. Rox's parents stare between the princes as Xair'uil's statement sinks in. Someone here must have told the Tabre where the ship was.

"Father, he saved my mate's life. I believe killing him would be an insult to the goddess herself. He is clearly blessed in luck," Rox states, taking my hand in his. "A fitting punishment would be to send him back to his mother's home planet. If luck is still on his side, he will survive before his extended family find him."

"No, fuck no. Kill me now. Don't fucking send me there!" Xair'uil growls out, fighting Strad and the guard who hold him down on his knees. "Fucking let me go!" His roar makes me jump, and I move closer to Rox.

"Take him to our cells while we make plans to send him home within a year when the next transport travels that way," Kutod demands and clicks his fingers. Xair'uil shouts and roars all the way out of the room, but then there is a bigger problem in the name of a brother.

"If I'm king, I can kill him, and I will. My brother deserved revenge, and I will not be called a liar," he sneers and looks at me in disgust. "And I want to fuck your pretty mate to teach you and her a fucking lesson about where women belong in our society," Croveik growls, pulling out his sword. He drops it onto the stone floor, and Astrid screams out a cry. "I challenge you, Prince Khirrox, for the throne. We meet on the ancient battlefield tomorrow at dawn."

Rox looks down at me as Astrid's cries fill the room, and my heart pangs in my chest. "I accept your challenge."

CHAPTER TWENTY-ONE

"So they are given one weapon at random and have to fight on top of a volcano?" I ask, summarizing what Marnie just told Savannah and me. Sav places her hand on mine on the table, and I get up, going back to pacing by the window that overlooks the city. It's been five hours since Rox accepted the challenge and quickly directed Kal to take me to his rooms and protect me with his life. Then he went with his other guards, quickly telling me something about training and that he will be back.

Sav and Marnie turned up an hour later after I'd thoroughly worn out the carpet with my pacing. I've hardly stopped for a moment to look at the rooms, the home Rox grew up in, because all I can feel is pure dread for what might come next.

"Basically, yes." Marnie nods. "Every king has beaten every contender or prince for the throne on that volcano. Only one king can step away, and any prince over the age of eighteen can initiate the challenge."

I think about it as I pace more, and Sav looks inches away from dragging my ass back to the chair. "Is Croveik known as a good fighter?"

"Sadly, yes, but Rox is a warrior, trained away from the court, and has fought many battles. All of Croveik's training has been inside the castle and against trainers who were frightened to touch the prince, so they let him win," Marnie reminds me.

"And I will not lose," Rox states, walking into the room and right up to me. Taking my face in his hands, he deeply kisses me, almost making me forget everything up to this point.

"We will go then," Sav awkwardly mumbles, and I hear Marnie agree and a door opening and shutting in the distance, but my main focus is on Rox.

"You can't leave me and die. You know that, right?" I say, pushing him towards the bedroom, kissing him harshly between every word. We get to the bed, and I gently push him back onto it. He lies back, looking up at me as I stand between his legs on the edge of the bed. I pull my top over my head and slowly push the rest of my clothes off until I'm naked and bare in front of him. His eyes run over my body in such a possessive way, almost like I can feel him claiming me with every single look.

"I will never leave you, my mate," he tells me as I undo his trousers and pull out his long hard cock into my hand. I love how his head falls back, and a sexy groan leaves his lips as I stroke him, feeling myself getting wet from just this. He doesn't have to touch me to make me want all of him.

"Never?" I question, climbing onto the bed and holding his cock right at my entrance. I meet his eyes as he looks up at me, his hands sliding up my outer thighs to my hips. "You just accepted a challenge to the death. Sounds like you want to leave me."

His hands slide up past my hips, brushing across my breasts, and I hold in a gasp. Finally, he cups the back of my neck and leans up, sinking fully inside me in the same movement. The pleasure is undeniable as he fills me and presses his lips onto mine, kissing me in a fevered passion. He pushes me onto my back, never pulling out of me, and moves swiftly to hold my hands over my head.

With each thrust, he drives home his next words. "I. Am. Not. Leaving. You. Ever."

I cry out as an orgasm slams into me, and I

tighten around Rox's thick cock, and he bites down on my shoulder as he comes, groaning against my skin. He rolls to my side, pulling me into his arms and kissing the top of my head.

"I will win this for you. For our future. My brother has always hated me and wanted everything I had. You are a prize he will not resist, and I won't let him touch you," he softly tells me. "I know you are worried, but I just found you. And I want to spend the rest of my life loving every inch of you."

"Rox...you will live longer than me. What happens when I die and you live for, what, two hundred more years?"

Rox grins at me, climbing on top of me and looking down as his already hard cock presses into my thigh. "When you're mated, you change. Your life is linked to mine now. You make me stronger. Finding a mate means I am no longer just one man fighting on my own. I have you, and you are the strongest woman I know."

"So we will die together tomorrow?" I question.

"No, my mate. We will live tomorrow and then forever." And then he thrusts into me, making me forget for a short time about the fact I could lose everything tomorrow.

THE CASTLE IS silent as I walk down the pathways, admiring how they wind and twist in places, the trees showing the way they want the castle built around them, and not the other way around like most places are. Kal stays close to my side, his hand constantly resting on his sword as it's clear we are not safe here. Rox left a few hours ago to prepare for the fight, and I know I can't be with him, I would just be a distraction at this point.

My emotions are all over the place. I flicker between pure panic and fear more often than not. I know whatever happens today, things are never going to be the same, and I'm not sure how to handle if it all goes badly. I'd die with Rox. I just know it. My soul cannot exist where he does not, and I don't care how crazy I must sound.

"Which way is it to the healer's area? I want to see someone called Zex," I ask Kal. He points the opposite way we just went, and we both turn around, and he leads this time.

"Zex is a good man. The queen herself has been helping care for his mate and child while he has been away," Kal tells me. "When the queen got sick, about five years ago, Zex was simply a healer in training, and he diagnosed the queen better than the royal healer did. It was how he got his job."

"There isn't a better man for it," I reply with a small smile, which I struggle to hold up. Smiling on the day my mate is going into a battle that could end in his death just doesn't feel right. We get to a pair of double doors with the word *healer* right above it, and Kal knocks once before we both walk inside.

I'm surprised to see Zex holding a little girl with bright green skin and curly silver hair in his arms, singing to her softly. On the other side of the room is my sister and an alien woman I don't know but suspect is Zex's mate. She is so pretty with big green eyes, long braided brown hair, and a curvy body hidden in blue robes. She turns to me the second I come in and instantly bows her head.

"Princess Darcie. It is an honour," she says, and Zex turns to me.

"It's just Darcie. I am a friend of your mate, but I cannot remember your name," I admit, quickly walking over to her. She smiles so brightly as she stands and stares at my hand I stretch out for her.

"My love, it's a human way of saying hello. They shake hands. All of us on the mission learned about it on Earth," Zex explains, and I see Sav's lips turn up in amusement as Zex's mate takes my hand and we awkwardly shake.

"Hello, my name is Zora," she tells me and lets my hand go. "Zex has told me so much about you and your story. You punched a Tabre wolf! You are so brave."

I sigh. "Everyone is going to remember that, aren't they?"

"Yes, wolf puncher," Zex replies around a quiet laugh, and Sav laughs with him. He hands the little girl back to her mother, and I peek at her, seeing how pretty she is. She has Zex's nose, but everything else is her mother's.

"What's her name?" I ask.

"Maryia," Zex tells me. "Isn't she perfect?"

"So perfect. I'm sorry to interrupt your time together, I just wanted to ask a question," I tell Zex.

"Gotta get in line, sis. I came here to ask something also," Sav interrupts.

"Why don't I take our little one to our rooms for a nap?" Zora gently suggests and leans up, kissing Zex softly once. The way he looks at her so adoringly makes me feel warm inside and think of Rox. "Come to us soon, love."

"Always," Zex tells her as she walks away and waves at us all. Kal moves to stand in front of the door when she is gone, and Zex looks between Sav and me.

"Who is going first then?"

"I'm the oldest," Sav suggests.

"Well, I'm a princess. That tops you," I reply with a grin.

"Princess Snooty Pants, should I tell Rox about that time you drove mum and dad's car into the lake with your first boyfriend and—"

"Okay, you go first," I blurt out before she can finish that sentence. Even the memory makes me cringe.

Sav smiles like the cat that got the mouse, and poor Zex looks uncomfortable. "So, I want to be a healer. Seems like a good job, and no women are healers on this planet as far as I can tell. I always wanted to be a doctor back on Earth, but it never worked out. So will you teach me? I'm eager to learn."

Zex looks surprised, and he rubs his chin, thinking on it for a moment. "You are correct, female healers are unheard of, but I am up for the challenge. I have never taken on an apprentice, but I have also not had a child I wish to spend all my time with. This would work well for us both."

"Then we have a deal," Sav says, and they shake hands before they both look at me.

"Well?" Sav gently asks.

"I've been feeling a little sick and wondered if you had anything to help. I just can't be sick at the battle today in front of everyone."

"It's likely nerves, right?" Sav says, walking closer and pulling me into a hug. "Rox will win this. He looks like he could crush his brother's head in his big hands, even without a weapon to help him."

"I would like to do a full check, but we do not have enough time right this moment. I suspect this is just a bad case of nerves, but here, drink this." He hands me a bottle of purple liquid. "This will help you relax somewhat, but know the people of Strixa are cheering for Rox and you."

"Thank you, my friend," I tell him, taking the bottle and giving him a quick hug. "And good luck with Sav. You just signed your soul to the devil."

"Hey!" Sav grumbles as I step back, and Zex laughs as he walks around us and leaves the room.

The moment I'm alone with my sister, the first tear falls, and then I can't stop myself from bursting into tears at the thought of losing Rox. She pulls me into her arms.

"It will be okay," she tells me, but her soothing words that used to make me feel better do nothing this time. All I can do is pray.

CHAPTER TWENTY-TWO

"Are you ready?" Rox asks me, stepping into the room as I finish putting on the dress his mother gave me to wear. The silky green material clings to my body, but somehow doesn't show too much, and it falls all the way to the floor. My hair is braided into a bun, with a few loose strands falling around the sides of my face, and I have green swirls painted down my cheek, past my neck and all the way to my wrists. Astrid sent two maids to help me paint them, and they both told me they are praying for Rox to win. It seems like the whole city, no, the whole planet is praying for my mate.

They must really hate Croveik as much as I do.

"No," I admit, turning around and seeing how his eyes glaze over as he looks me up and down. I can also feel his desire like it's my own, and it always is when I'm around Rox. Taking large steps, he walks right up to me and kisses me softly. His lips brush against mine, and I can't help pulling away to ask an important question.

"You will fight for me today. Right?" I ask him, cupping his cheek. "I need you to win for me, or I am dying with you."

"I swear to the goddess I will fight for you forever," he firmly tells me and leans down, kissing me one more time before stepping back and offering me his hand. "We have transportation waiting on us."

"Okay," I breathe out, feeling like I am the one going to a battle instead of Rox. I guess it's a sure way of knowing he is taking my heart and soul with him. We head down the pathways surrounded by a group of guards, including Strad and Kal who look very on edge. It takes us about ten minutes to get outside the castle where four very fancy cars are waiting on the cobblestone ground. They are black, smooth and sleek, and the doors literally disappear away when we get close. Sav and Marnie are with Zex, and we pass them as we head for the first car. Sav smiles at me, but I don't respond, knowing my sister could always see right through me. I always relied on her to be the strong one for all of us, but right now? I need to find my own strength for what comes next.

Rox and I get into the sleek car, and the door just reappears. Damn, that's some advanced tech.

"Chloe would love this car and everything about it," I tell Rox as the car starts, barely making any noise. "And as much as I want to find them, I'm never leaving your side. I'm choosing you, and you are going to win this for me."

"It is a promise," he tells me, lifting my hand and kissing the back as the car takes off. "And we will find your sisters. The galaxy couldn't hide the Jackson sisters for long."

"I hope not," I whisper, leaning my head on Rox's shoulder and watching the city pass by in the blur.

FOR A PLANET of mostly green pretty shit, the burning hot red volcano sure is an eyesore. It took us about two hours to travel across forests to the volcano, and now I can do nothing but stand by my mate's side as he waits for his father to place two weapons in the middle of the clearing inside the volcano. The king gets to choose the weapons and will be the one who starts the fight and announces the winner by giving them the crown as it his sons. It doesn't matter that one of them is adopted. He is still a prince. As I understand it, the current king can choose to fight the winner, but he has already said he will stand down. Only the current king is allowed to do so, forfeiting the fight in a way that everyone wins. Strad moves to my other side, and Rox looks to him and nods once.

"What is that about?" I narrow my eyes at them both.

"In case I am badly injured and not dead. My brother will try to keep me alive to watch as he takes you from me. I will not let that happen," Rox explains, and I get it now. Strad is an escape plan for me. Tears fill my eyes as I glare up at my mate.

"We both leave this damn volcano, or neither of us will," I convey to him, and he smirks, making my heart feel warm inside my chest.

"You faced a wolf and punched it in the face with little training. I will deal with my brother," he tells me, and I smile for a moment. Just a moment. That's all we get before a loud sound blasts in the distance, and I look behind me at the crowd gathered on the edges of the volcano, looking down, watching this fight which could destroy the only man I have ever loved.

The only man I will ever love.

"Win this, and you play the wolf tonight and bite me," I tell him, and he laughs, though it doesn't all stretch to his eyes before he lets me go as I whisper one more sentence that hurts to say. "I love you." Strad gently grabs my arm when I go to follow him, and I try not to cry. A delicate hand finds mine on my other side, and I turn to see Astrid.

"Vyuna placed each of my children in my hands for different reasons, but I love them each the same. Despite the choices they have made and the monster they have fed inside their hearts, they are my children. I have made many mistakes, but Rox...he is my proudest creation," she softly tells me. I briefly look over to see Rox and Croveik standing opposite each other, and the king stands between them, telling them something while holding two axes that shine red. "My kind little boy who looked at the stars like they were not dying but just waiting for the right person to save them."

"I'm sorry," I whisper to her and feel my hand warming. I look down. "I don't know how to feel your pain, but I imagine I will one day. My mum always said children are a gift you are given and have to give back one day. But you never stop loving them, protecting them, and that is the gift that always stays for them."

"You are with child, I sense it," she whispers to me, but I see Strad turn our way as I try not to fall over in shock. Astrid holds me tightly to her side as I suck in a breath, and a smile forms on my lips despite everything. "A strong child. You are blessed by Vyuna herself."

"Thank you, Vyuna," I say, breathing the prayer into the air around us as drums start to play a heavy beat, echoing around us. "Now please keep my mate alive."

Thoughts of a baby flicker to the back of my mind as the king walks towards us and takes his place on the other side of Astrid. I look back to see Croveik spitting words at Rox, and I can't make any of them out, but he looks mad. Something has ticked him off. I run my eyes over Rox's bare back and long legs that are only hidden from the knee upwards in a ceremonial robe. Our mating marks look like they are on fire on his back, the flames of the fire around us creating that effect.

The world seems to slow as the king shouts a word I don't recognise into the air, and the fight begins. They both run for the axes, crashing into each other, and I gasp as Croveik manages to get his first and sweeps a cut across Rox's arm. Rox recovers quickly as he gets his own axe and blocks the next hit. Rox elbows Croveik hard in the face, and even from this distance, I hear the snap of his nose. He screams as he stumbles back, spitting blood onto the floor where it sizzles from the heat. The crowd applauds and shouts, the sound mixing with the drums and echoing so loudly around the whole place that it feels like it mixes with my own heart as I watch every tiny movement that Rox makes.

They violently slam into each other with the axes, nibbling each other's skin every time one of them swings around. No one gets a good hit in, but just watching them makes me feel sick. Rox is amazing, dodging each move and blocking any that get close, but Croveik is too polished, too perfect. Rox moves quicker than him suddenly, slamming his axe down on Croveik, who blocks it, but Rox uses his axe like a pole and throws himself over Croveik, landing behind him. In one smooth swing, he slams his axe at Croveik's side, and it goes all the way through his stomach. Blood splatters everywhere, smothering Rox like a wave and littering the ground. The heat makes the blood steam up, creating a mist around them, and the crowd goes silent. I stare in shock as Rox kneels down at his brother's side, blood dripping from his hair, and closes his brother's eyes.

Queen Astrid bursts into tears, and I pull her into my arms, meeting King Kutod's eyes over her shoulder, and I see the sorrow in his eyes.

"Axe fighting has always been Rox's strength," he tells me, but it means so much more. He wanted Rox to win. I smile sadly at him, and he clears his throat before walking to Rox. I watch as King Kutod kneels down in front of Rox and takes his crown off before offering it to Rox. Rox looks over at me as he takes the crown, then coats it in blood before lifting it and placing it on his head. The crowd cheers, but I only watch as Rox places his hand on his father's shoulder before walking to me. Astrid lets go of me to run to her dead son's side, kneeling with her husband, but I hardly notice as Rox pulls me into his arms.

"I felt your strength like we were one," Rox tells me, leaning back, and he takes his crown from his head and places it on me. The crowd erupts in roars of approval. "And from this moment on, we are."

CHAPTER TWENTY-THREE

Holding the tiny purple baby in my arms as she sleeps makes me wonder exactly what my twins will look like. Marnie's daughter, Lily-Anne, is just the sweetest little baby I have ever seen. She looks just like Marnie, with her locks of hair and her mum's eyes, but she has the skin colour of her father.

"Queen Darcie," Kal speaks quietly behind me, and I turn back to him. "Your sister has made another guard cry due to rejection and is causing a scene in the royal healer's rooms. May I be excused to sort the situation? There are five other guards in the area, and one will replace me. I believe Strad is near."

"Send Strad and tell my sister to stop breaking hearts," I sigh, trying not to laugh. A brief deep chuckle escapes Kal, and I can't stop the laugh that fills my throat from coming out as he bows and walks away. I catch a reflection of myself in the mirror behind where Kal was, and I think I look a million times different from the poor farm girl I was only a year ago. I now have curly blonde hair that is shiny and long, my skin is slightly tanned from the sun here, and my crown glows a faint green light over my face, matching my green eyes. My mother's necklace sits on my neck, matching the bracelet from Astrid on my wrist, and it makes me feel loved to see them. I see my mating marks shining in the light, the beautiful swirls almost glittering in the sunshine and making me think of my mate.

But most of all, I see my little baby bump peeking out of my dress.

Marnie walks over to me from the other side of the royal gardens, not far from the rooms she lives in as my lady in waiting. I remember when I asked Marnie to be my lady in waiting, a high up place for any woman in the court, and it means she is at my side in the day and lives in the castle. I couldn't think of anyone else I know who would like to live here and could be trusted completely. Marnie didn't blink before saying yes and moving in the very same day with her mate, only a month before this little one turned up.

"Not long now until there will be three babies between us," Marnie says as she sits next to me on the grass. This part of the castle is separate from the rest where Astrid and Kutod live, and Rox has helped me turn it into a home I just love. We have four rooms we mostly live in and a new nursery that Rox painted himself to look like stars on the ceiling.

"Twin girls. I'm so excited to meet them," I admit, stroking Lily-Anne's little hand sticking out the white blanket. I hand Marnie her baby back before stretching my legs out and stumbling to my feet with my giant bump. Five months with twins? It hurts your back, and you can't have alien sex all the time. It sucks. But it's so going to be worth it when it is all over.

I say goodbye to Marnie before making my way back to my rooms, surprised to see the door open when I get close. I head inside and see Astrid sitting on the couch next to Rox. She hugs Rox as I walk in, and her eyes snap to me.

"How are you?!" she exclaims, hurrying off the sofa and rushing to me. I hug my mother-in-law, who I see as a second mother now, before making my way to my mate.

"Grumpy," I admit to Astrid who chuckles.

"Some pregnancies can be difficult," she softly

tells me. "I will leave you with your mate to relax for the evening."

"Are you free tomorrow? I could use some advice on the flowers I'm planting on our balcony," I ask her, and her face lights up.

"I am! I will call round tomorrow mid-day!" she squeals and leaves the room not long after. Rox holds his arm out for me, and I sit down, snuggling into his side.

"You make my mother very happy," he tells me. "Thank you."

"I like her," I tell him as he rests his hands on my bump, his large hands covering most of the bump. "She is kind and honest. I see where you got those traits from."

I smile as one of the babies kicks Rox's hand, and I see the look of adoration in his eyes. Our daughters are going to be so loved...and Vyuna help them when they find their own mates. Overprotective dad mode might be sexy for me though.

"I wish I had better news for you about your sisters. There is still no news, bad or good," he tells me, looking stressed. For the first time, I realise how hard this must be on him.

"You know I don't regret you taking me or blame you for not finding them. I believe we all have our own fates, and I will see all my sisters again one day," I tell him, cupping his cheek with my hand.

"I should have taken your sisters on board with you and not left them," he tells me. "They would be safe."

"It wasn't meant to be," I remind him. "We talk about fate all of the time, and I've grown to accept things happen for a reason. Plus, we Jackson sisters are not weak, and I know you are doing everything you can. Alice...I worry about her." I pause, my voice catching. I have to believe that whoever has her wants her alive and will give her the medicine she needs. I can't imagine her dead. I won't ever think it. "But we will find them. Sav is going to search the galaxy and set all the planets on fire until she finds them. I just know it."

"We will help her, even if we cannot leave the planet for some time," he replies and leans down, kissing me softly, and his lips drift to my bump and then a little lower. "Can I convince you to spend the evening in our bedroom?"

"Naked?" I taunt, climbing onto his lap. Despite my literal bump between us, I feel closer every day to Rox. Finding my mate was exactly what I was searching for.

"Yes, Queen Darcie. You are needed for royal duties," he teases, stroking his hands down my chest.

I laugh as he swiftly picks me up and carries me to the bedroom. I found my forever when I won the Lottery, and I would never change a thing.

"You have to see this, Sav," Darcie's horrified voice fills my ears as I finish checking on one of the patients in the healing water, and the green woman smiles softly at me. I don't regret for one second begging Zex to train me how to be a healer. I frown, turning around as Darcie waddles into the room, and Rox, her loving mate, comes running after her like the big green giant he is.

"You shouldn't be running with twins at eight months pregnant!" I shout, telling her off, but when I see the tears in her eyes, I look down at the tablet in her small shaking hands where a video plays.

"Earth is burning. I can't tell you anything else, but we are seeing several tears in space, and dragon-

like creatures are pouring out of the cracks. They are taking over the planet. We cannot get in contact with Earth, and we are in a ship passing by. This is the only footage we have." The picture changes from a green-skinned panicked alien to an image of Earth like I've never seen it. Massive purple cracks fill the space around the Earth, and it burns red where the land used to be. Two creatures can be seen, huge dragons the size of cars, with silver scales fly right down to Earth.

"Oh my god. Isabelle! Is she on the transport?" I demand, meeting Darcie's eyes as she shakes her head, and my heart drops.

No, no, no, no.

"The ship won't arrive for another two months," she whispers, and I shake my head, my back smacking into the medical unit. I didn't even realise I was falling until I hit it.

"She has to be alive. Isabelle is smart and...and...," I drift off, stumbling over my words. Rox picks Darcie up, cradling her as she bursts into tears, and I meet his eyes. Darcie passes out, a common thing for her at this stage of pregnancy when there is too much stress. I watch how Rox looks down at her and holds her to his chest.

True love is real, and I've been lucky enough to

see it.

"I have to leave today. You must have a ship and some men, right?" I demand of him, crawling to my feet. I lower my voice. "Please."

"It will not be safe. We have fought those creatures before," he reminds me. I know their history; I've been living here for months. "But I will not stand in your way. You may take the royal ship. Find Strad on the docking floor and tell him to prepare the ship."

"Thank you!" I say, looking once at Darcie, so small in his arms, before meeting Rox's gaze. "Protect my sister. I will come back, and if you don't, this human is going to be your worst nightmare."

"She is my queen, the mother of my soon-to-be born twin children, and most importantly my mate. I would die before any harm becomes her," he tells me, and I believe him. Considering I don't trust men at all, it must mean he is a good man. Anyone that puts up with Darcie is a saint in my books anyway. I stroke my sister's cheek before running out of the room, grabbing my medical bag on the way out. I rush down the corridors of the castle, moving in and out of the archways before getting to the elevators.

This place is a maze mixed with modern tech and old stuff.

And I love it.

The elevator doors open, and I step in, pressing the button for the docking floor below. Just before the elevator closes, a blue hand stops the doors, and jolting pain hits me hard in my stomach. I hold my stomach, even though there is nothing there as a blue-skinned alien man steps into the elevator, looking like a sexy blue model with wide shoulders, toned body and tattoos peeking out of the rips on his shirt. His blond hair is the colour of ash and messily mixes in with the slight blond beard he has going on. His ears are high and tipped, and if I remember right, he is from the planet Noveta.

He pauses, slowly looking me over from bottom to top before smirking.

It's only then that I notice the handcuffs hanging from his wrist, and the green blood on his black clothes. And the cuts on his skin.

The doors shut as I slam my back against the wall, and alarms start going off in the distance.

The man never once takes his eyes off me as he lifts his hand gripping a gun and points it at my chest. I didn't even notice he had a gun on him.

"I need to get out of here, and you're coming with me as my hostage. I need a female to break into my planet. The name's Xair. Now move."

The End For Now.

To read Savannah and Xair's book, click here.

GLOSSARY

Planet Strixa

Capital City- Satita, the first city of green light.

Home of the green-skinned Ixa race with incredible strength.

Planet Noveta

Unknown capital city.

Home of the blue-skinned Nova race who can run faster than any other race.

Planet Idillon

Capital City- Ilros, the city born of a thousand light stars.

Home of the purple-skinned Illon race who can hear for miles.

Planet Giea

Capital City- Oasisa, the water city.

Home of the silver-skinned Gie race who can breathe underwater.

Planet Tabrerth

Unknown capital city.

Home of the gold-skinned Tabre race who can control and talk to animals.

Planet Earth

Currently under invasion.

Home of the Earthlings/humans with incredible compassion.

Planet Dragonria

Home of the Dragonmir race. Unknown gifts.

VYUNA, GODDESS OF THE HARVEST, BRIEF STORY

Vyuna is the goddess of the Harvest, and Vyuna and her nameless mate created the universe for each other. Every planet was a gift, and each gift was better than the last. From strength to speed to long lives, the gifts spread across the universe like a wave, each race receiving a special power unique to that planet. Their love spanned thousands, if not millions, of years until Vyuna grew bored with the worlds that had no life. In her misery, her mate stabbed himself in the heart and flew around the planets, bleeding life into the worlds for her to love.

The words written on the base of every statue of Vyuna are:

"We create worlds for those we love."

Vyuna died at the same time as her mate, unable to stand life without him in it. They loved each other deeply, and it was the first real mating. Now many people can mate, finding those who are destined for each other, for the true magic of the universe is found in mating.

ABOUT THE AUTHOR

Vivian Star is a fantasy author from the U.K. To hear about new releases sign up to my newsletter here.

Link to Newsletter.

When you start living with your four overprotective brothers for the first time, the smart thing is to avoid their extremely hot best friend, and not kiss him. Right?

Izzy King knows dating former playboy, Blake Frost, behind her family's back isn't the greatest idea.

When the attraction becomes too great to avoid, keeping their relationship a secret is the only way they can be together.

But, Izzy isn't the only one keeping secrets. The King brothers are full of them.

Can Blake and her brothers keep her safe from the past that haunts them all?

These kings could destroy her, but she isn't able to walk away…Danger, lust, and King brothers never mix well.

18+ due to violence, sexual scenes, and language.

Blake doesn't say anything to defend himself, not that words would really help at this point. Sebastian rushes forward and punches him in the face as I watch in horror. They wrestle onto the ground, and Blake blocks most of Sebastian's punches, using his arms to cover his face. Yet, he doesn't fight back, or even try to stop Sebastian at all. It's like he wants this as punishment, like he thinks he deserves to suffer for loving me.

"She's my fucking sister, not one of your little fuck buddies!" Sebastian sneers, managing to knock Blake's arm away and landing a sickening punch.

Other people run into the room at the commotion. I look up to see Elliot, followed by Luke and Harley. I don't take my eyes away from Sebastian and Blake for more than a second though. Blake still defends himself but won't fight back, while Sebastian tries to get more hits in.

"Stop them!" I shout at my other brothers, with tears running down my cheeks. My shouting finally snaps Harley out of his shock, and he pushes between them, holding Sebastian back from Blake.

"What's going on? Calm the fuck down, Seb," Harley says calmly, but I can see the threat in the way he stands, holding both of Sebastian's arms at his sides.

"I love her. I'm in love with your sister, and I'm not the least bit sorry," Blake states, and his blue eyes meet mine.

CHAPTER TWENTY-FOUR

IZZY

"Elizabeth, come downstairs!" the angry voice of my foster dad rings through the house. Groaning, I look over at my clock, only to see it's five in the morning. I was hoping for it to be at least seven. I have four hours until school, but I know I'll have to clean the whole damn house before I can leave. I roll out of bed to have a quick shower and throw on jeans, a vest, and a hoodie before running down the stairs. Stopping at the mirror in the hallway, I pause to pull my long, almost-white hair into a ponytail and hoping it doesn't look too messy. The two-bedroom house is a tip, despite the fact I cleaned it yesterday morning, like I do most mornings. Fred, my *lovely* foster dad, is passed out on a stool in the kitchen with his hand wrapped around a vodka bottle. He must have passed out sometime during my shower. I know better than to talk to him, it's not worth waking him up and making him angry. So, I start cleaning around him quietly.

They kept me up most of the night with their loud music and another party that didn't stop until three in the morning. *Let's not mention the idiots who tried to open my locked door.* I guess I should be thankful they, at least, feed me for doing the cleaning. I know that if I didn't get up and clean, there would be no food for a week.

Finally, at eight, it's all done. I grab my bag, slamming the door on my way out.

As much as I try to forget my living situation, I can't, because every day is a reminder. I've lived with Fred and Vivian since I was fifteen. It's been a nightmare from day one. Sure, they act all lovely and great when social services are around, but, in reality, they use me to clean the house. I just try to stay out of their way. I have six more months until I'm eighteen, and then I can leave. I'm not sure where, but honestly, anywhere would be better. I have no living family and no money, so I don't have many options other than to find a job quickly and a room to rent.

I walk into school thirty minutes later, a little hot

from the warm weather we have been enjoying. I glance around at the grammar school which I have to attend. It's this or college, supposedly the grammar school is good for my grades. *But, I have always felt it's more like the better of two evils.*

The day progresses as I would usually expect it to, filled with art and history classes all day. I took a double-A level in art and one in history, which is surprisingly not that boring.

Later that day, as I sit at lunch alone like every day, I think of my best friend, Tilly. She moved to France two months ago and was the only reason I could deal with this crazy-ass school. It's full of posh idiots whose parents paid to get them in, not like me and Tilly, who actually get straight A's. Tilly really didn't need to study hard like I did, but she did anyway, and that's why I like her.

I'm pulled from my thoughts by the intercom. "Would Elizabeth Turner come to the main office?"

When it clicks off, I look up to see everyone staring at me. I shrug as I try not to blush. *I hate being the centre of attention.*

I walk to the office on the other side of the building after getting my things. I keep thinking of what the hell I've done or if Fred has called to say there is another family emergency at home. Which is usually code for '*I have friends coming to get drunk, and I need the house clean again and didn't notice you had already cleaned.*' I roll my eyes and soon I'm at the office, where I'm told to go straight in by the snooty receptionist.

I walk into the room to see my head teacher behind the desk and the back of a tall man with dark-brown hair tied in a loose knot at the back of his head, who's standing in front of the desk.

"Come and sit, Elizabeth, there has been some news, and this man has come to talk to you," says my head teacher, but I ignore him and watch as the dark-haired man turns to me.

"It's nice to meet you. You wouldn't believe how long I have looked for you, and it's a little bit of a shock to finally meet my sister," the stranger says to me in a deep voice.

Wait, sister?

I turn and look at my head teacher, hoping he will help, but he ignores me and looks out the window. *I guess this is as awkward for him as it is for me.* I look back at the man, taking in his head of dark-brown hair and massive, muscular build and his expensive looking pressed suit. I finally look into his eyes and see the same bright-green eyes I have, which are looking back at me.

I gasp and start to back away into a seat on the couch. I look down at the floor as I try to collect my thoughts. My mother never told me anything about my father, just that I wouldn't want to meet him and left it at that. She passed away a few years ago, four days after my fifteenth birthday. I guessed she would have told me about him when I was older, but who knows? *She never got the chance.*

"Look, I know this is strange, but I am your half-brother, and I have custody of you until you turn eighteen. I've come to take you back home with me. Family means everything to me, and once I heard you were in a foster home... I can't leave here without taking you home. To a real family."

He states it like it's an everyday fact that you just find your sister and demand she come and live with you. *Not that it's weird as hell.* I look him over, again, seeing his neutral expression, how he waits for my answer silently. I get the impression not a lot bothers him, and I've only just met him. I have a brother, and if that isn't enough to deal with, he wants me to move. *I should panic and run, god knows who this man actually is.* Who knows what he wants or if he is even my brother, but, then again, it can't be worse than where I live now. I doubt the headmaster would have let him anywhere near me if he didn't have some kind of proof.

"Proof, do you have proof?" I ask.

"Yes," the man claiming to be my brother says. He walks to the desk, picking up a folder and handing it to me. I skim through most of it, but it's true. This man somehow has my birth records, a DNA test that was done when I was a baby, and it has my mother's signature on it. *Holy crap, I have family. I'm not alone.*

"Elizabeth, look at me," my brother gently asks as I close the folder and put it down on a nearby chair. I look up into those familiar, green eyes, which show me some kindness. I try to think of more reasons to run, but it seems pointless. *Well, I think I'm going to have to trust him.*

"It's Izzy, my friends call me Izzy. What's your name?" I ask him.

I'm still looking at his face, trying to see the truth behind his words. I get the feeling he is a closed book as far as emotions go, but I can see some kindness, and that's enough for me to try to relax.

"I'm Harley King, nice to meet you Izzy." He smiles, and it takes me a minute to realise he kind of looks like I do in pictures when I smile.

I stand up quickly, putting some distance

between us because it's a little bit too much. "What did you mean when you said you would take me back with you, and custody?" I try to ask calmly and kind of fail when my voice is high-pitched and squeaky as I talk. *Real smooth, Izzy.*

"I meant that you're coming to live with me, as you have no other blood relatives as far as I know. I have custody of you, so it's all above board. I have custody of my three younger brothers, too," he pauses, "well, your brothers, too." I watch as he scratches his head with a huff, and he sits down on the sofa and straightens his suit jacket before saying, "I know this is hard for you to believe, and *trust me,* this whole situation is difficult.

"Our father is dead. I took over when he died. I was twenty, and the twins, Sebastian and Elliot, were fifteen. Luke was fourteen. It was difficult, but I made it work. I later found out—from a letter from Dad's will—about you. It had the results of a DNA test done when you were a baby, and an old address and number of yours. Of course, it's taken me two years to find you due to all the moves you, and your mother, had taken." He stops talking and looks up to meet my eyes, "I'm sorry for your loss by the way."

I nod and sit next to him, taking it all in. *I have four brothers.* I guess he is right about us moving when I think about it. My mother just liked to see new places, and I was taken along for the ride. Yesterday, I had no one, now I have a family, and I am moving away from my crazy, foster family. *This shit seems unbelievable.*

"All right, I'm going to be honest with you. I've done everything I can to leave my crazy, foster parents. So, this could work for me. I mean, moving to your place, and then we can see how things go. I guess I would like to meet the rest of you and learn about you. How old are my brothers now?" I ask, looking at Harley, who looks around twenty-three. *So, they can't be that old.*

"The twins are seventeen, like you, and Luke is sixteen. I'm so glad you'll come. I thought I'd have a massive fight on my hands with getting you to come with me," he says with a grin, which makes me smile too.

He stands up, claps his hands together, getting the attention of my head teacher, and starts talking to him about sending my paperwork over for the switching of my school. I notice he makes a very a large payment to the school to help hurry up my paperwork. I look at him now, in his perfect suit, and frown. I glance down at my baggy hoodie and shabby jeans then finally to my worn trainers I have had for at least two years. *I'm not going to fit into their world.*

As we head to my house in his massive, black SUV–which is shinier than most of the cars in my small town–I sit wondering what Harley will think of my foster parents or their home. Let's hope the place doesn't still smell like vodka when we get there.

CHAPTER TWENTY-FIVE

"Izzy, we need to go soon. I understand if you want to wait until tomorrow to pack and say your good-byes," Harley comments while pulling the car into the parking space next to the house.

I sit back and glance around at the house I've spent part of my life living in. The front of the house has long grass, which is mostly weeds, covering the small, front lawn and cracked pavement leading to the door. The house, itself, hasn't been worked on for years, and it's clear from the outside. My lazy, and possibly crazy, foster parents wouldn't bother leaving the house to do any work on it. Well, they didn't care enough to make me mow it or risk neighbours seeing me working my ass off for them. It's a nice neigh-bourhood with decent people living here, and they need to keep up some kind of appearance. So many memories are bad here, but also, in some ways, this place made me stronger.

"No. I only have a bag of things. So it will only take me half an hour to pack. Do you want to wait?" I ask, hoping he will stay. I secretly don't want to be alone with them when they find out I'm leaving. They have never hurt me, but throwing things near me and screaming at me is normal for them. Frowning, I think of times when it had been worse when they'd been drinking, which I'm guessing they have been by now. *It is midday*.

"Yes. I need to tell them about you leaving with me," he tells me and then frowns. "Well, your foster parents should have received a phone call or letter explaining anyway." He hesitates as he stares at the house. "Why have you only got one bag? What about your clothes and, well, girl stuff?" he asks while pulling out the car keys.

I nearly sigh in relief that he's not leaving me here, and I reply quietly, "I don't have many clothes or other things." I try to get out of the car, not wanting to discuss this anymore, but a large hand on my upper arm gently stops me. He huffs, bringing my attention back to him as he moves his hand.

"Seb is going to love spoiling you with my credit

card. Money has never been a problem for us, and you might hate us for spoiling you, but we are going to," he says with a cheeky grin, and then he laughs loudly as he gets out of the car.

I frown at his statement about spending so much money on me, but my nerves get the best of me and don't let me think about it anymore. I straighten up and walk into the house, with Harley following me. We walk into the living room, where my foster dad is passed out, face-down on the sofa with a bottle of vodka in his hand. I'm guessing Vivian is at one of her friends', as she is nowhere to be seen.

"I wouldn't wake him up if I was you. I'll go and pack," I say in a whisper, shrugging at Harley as he glares at Fred on the sofa. He looks around the room in disgust before smiling at me with a look of pity behind his gaze.

As I walk past him, he tells me to hurry up. I suppress a smile at that and run up to my room. I throw my three pairs of jeans, four tops, and my leggings into a bag. I get all of my underwear and the necklace my mother gave me. It's the only thing my foster parents haven't sold of mine. The memory of my mother comes rushing at me as I hold the necklace.

I know I shouldn't be looking in Mum's jewellery

box, but everything is so pretty. I'm only seven, so Mum won't be too mad. I open the worn, wooden box, and inside are pretty, little earrings I've seen my mom wear, and, in the middle, is a very pretty, purple necklace I've never seen. I pull it out, holding it up in the air as it sparkles in the light from the window, making me giggle.

"Elizabeth," the angry voice of my mother makes me jump and turn, and I see her standing in the doorway. Her white-blond hair is up in a messy bun from cleaning, and she is wearing a pretty, red dress.

Her face softens slightly before she lets out a long breath and comes over to me. She kneels in front of the stool I'm sitting on and takes the necklace out of my hand gently.

"It's real pretty, Mummy," I say, frowning at my mummy's sad face.

"It is, isn't it? I haven't looked at this in years. It's called a sapphire," she tells me.

"Who gave you it, Mummy?" I ask as she stares at the necklace in her hand. The sapphire is about the size of her thumb and shines like my mummy's blue eyes.

"The man who still holds my heart, baby. I just can't let this go," she whispers the end part to herself,

then she stands up, putting the necklace back into her box and holding her hand out to me.

"Do you want to go and get ice cream? Mummy could use some chocolate ice cream," she smiles, making me laugh.

"Yes, Mummy," I squeal, jumping up and down.

The memory of her fades, leaving only the sadness that she is gone. I kept it hidden well enough because of that memory. I guess I had always hoped it was my dad who gave it to her, but who knows? It looks expensive, but my mum never dated anyone, that I saw when growing up, so it could be. *I could ask Harley.* I put it into my bag and then go into the bathroom to collect my shampoos, soap, razors, and hairbrush. I chuck those into the bag and look at myself in the full-length mirror.

My long, almost white-blond hair is nearly at my waist. Even in a plait like it is now. I have those bright-green eyes, like my brother, and a layer of freckles, of which I'm not a fan. I'm quite pale, as I don't get out much, but I have a good body. *As my best friend would tell me anyway.* I'm looking at my eyes, wondering about my father, when I hear a thump and a man cry out. I race down the stairs, finding Harley holding Fred by his neck up against a wall, and Harley's face is close to Fred's.

"Don't speak about my sister like that ever again, or I'll end you. Do you understand me?" he asks.

Fred mumbles a shaken, "Yes."

Harley lets him drop to the floor. He looks back at me with a smile and starts brushing down his suit before asking, "You ready?" I nod, and he turns back to Fred with a scary amount of hate on his face.

"We're going now, and don't contact my sister or I'll find you."

With that, he gestures for me to walk out, and I do so with my head held high. I say goodbye to my old life and head out into the new.

CHAPTER TWENTY-SIX

We drive for nearly seven hours toward the Lake District, away from my old life. Harley tells me that we'll be living in a small village called Kendean, where they are all from. Harley continues, telling me I will be joining the twins in their last year at the local grammar school. The school does the same courses that I am doing now, and I can continue them for the few remaining months I have left. We talk about what I study, and I tell him about my love of art and history. I also tell Harley I want to work with my art when I'm older. I'm surprised when he thinks this is a great idea and can't wait to see my work.

"So, what work do you do?" I ask.

"I own the local gym in the village. It's the only

one for miles so we do good business. Plus, it helps that we all had a very good inheritance." He glances at me before looking back at the road.

"That's why you're so buff then," I joke, and he grins at me.

"Yes, and so are your brothers. You can come any time to build some muscles if you want," he smiles.

"No, I don't do exercise." I laugh at his shocked face. "I'm serious. I can run if I want to, but I get all red and sweaty. Well, I'm lazy."

"You're joking, right? Don't you eat? Because you're quite thin and small," his tone is now serious.

I can understand why, seeing where I came from, but I'm just lucky I have a good body despite not doing much exercise. *My friend, Tilly, always used to moan about that.*

"I just have good genes, I guess. I have a bad addiction to Ben and Jerry's ice cream."

I laugh with Harley when he answers, "It's good that Luke likes that stuff and it's always in the freezer, then."

"I may like Luke already," I say.

"Do you drive? We live in the middle of nowhere and, without a car, it will be difficult to get around," he says, and I sigh, thinking back to Tilly's father who bought me a crash course for my seventeenth birthday from all of them. It was the sweetest thing, even if I could never afford a car and insurance. I passed straight away out of pure luck, I believe, and a few late nights practising in my foster parents' car.

"Yeah, I have a licence," I answer.

"That's great, all the boys have cars, so one of us will be able to drive you anywhere until Sebastian or I can buy you a new car," he tells me.

"That's too much money," I frown.

Harley laughs at that and we carry on the drive in a comfortable silence. As we pull into the village, we cross over a beautiful, old bridge with a large river running through the town. As we drive farther, I notice the small mountains in the background. The town is beautiful, even at night. Glancing at the clock on the dash, I realize it's now close to midnight, and I hope to go straight to bed when we get there. *I'm glad we stopped off for some food on the road.*

We pass more country roads and eventually pull onto a small road with heavy, black gates, which are open. I can see a long road behind them with massive trees on both sides, and it's lit up with large, street lamps.

Harley mutters something about the gates being open when they weren't meant to be and drives up the path. Slowly, the biggest house I've ever seen comes into view. It's beautiful, grey stone, even in dim lighting, but all the cars parked in front and the loud music blasting from inside distracts me it.

I wonder if this is normal. I briefly think I have no chance of sleeping until morning as I look at the garage built on the side of the house and then the people flittering around outside. I can't see much in the dark, but big windows seem to line the front of the house.

"For fuck's sake, I leave them for three days and come back to a massive party," Harley shouts in frustration as he jumps out of the car and slams the door.

I go to follow, and he gestures for me to stay behind him. I really wouldn't want to be my brothers right now. *Harley looks scary as hell.* He slams the massive, wooden doors open and pushes drunken people out of the way as I follow him. I can't see or hear much over the amount of people and noise from the loudspeakers, which make my ears feel like they are bleeding. I haven't been to many parties because I just didn't have the clothes or the time to go to them.

We pass through a dark kitchen, which has three couples making out on the counters. I keep my head down and try not to look around. I do spot the booze everywhere when we pass through a dining room, where there were teenagers dancing on the impressive, wooden table. We eventually make our way into a living area, with two massive speakers, one on either side of the largest TV I've ever seen. A music channel, with nearly naked girls dancing, is flashing across the screen. There are three black-leather sofas spread around the TV, with a couple on each of them. The room is dark, so I can't see much more.

Harley leans into me to shout. "I'm going to turn the electric off in the basement. Stay here, if anyone bothers you, tell them you're with me, all right?" He sighs. "I'm so sorry about this, Izzy." He tells me with a frown, taking off his jacket and throwing it onto a sofa next to a couple who don't even notice.

I nod. "No problem, go."

I lean against a wall next to the window in the lounge, looking out into the massive garden with a huge tree in the middle. There are lights all up the tree, highlighting a big tree house. The tree house currently has drunken people in it, and I watch as two bottles fall off and smash when they hit the ground.

Harley's going to kill our brothers.

It's strange saying 'our brothers' when I'm used to having no one. My thoughts stop when large hands circle around my waist and pull me up against a hard chest. I look up, turn around, and push my hands into the chest of a massive man. He's maybe a little shorter than Harley, but he is still impressive, with wavy, dirty-blond hair and a handsome face. He is gorgeous, even my ex, Devon, wasn't this attractive. The man is wearing a tight, grey shirt and blue jeans, with a surfer-guy kind of look going on, and, holy crap, he has amazing muscles.

My hands tremble as I push them into his chest to push him away, but I'm only fooling myself as my hands want to stay there. The pretty guy grins at me and leans down even as I feel the hard muscles under my hands.

As his warm hands go to my hips, he says, "I haven't seen you before, and, trust me, I would remember. What's your name, beauty?" he asks in a deep, seductive voice that makes my body shiver, and not because it's cold.

I haven't been attracted to anyone since Devon, and, well, he was great. *This guy has my stomach and nipples tightening from just one sentence.* I bet he knows it because my boobs are pushed against his chest, a downside of being big chested.

"None of your business," I sigh and clear my throat. "Look, I'm here with Harley, and I'm just waiting for him. So, you should let go," I say as calmly as I can. I hope not to show my husky tone as my hands are still on his chest, and his hands are still on my hips running circles with his thumbs. *This is turning me on, and I need to control myself.*

"Harley is out of town, or this party wouldn't be happening. So, try again, beauty. What's your name? Or will I just have to keep calling you 'beauty'?" He grins and two beautiful dimples appear. *How did I not notice these before?*

"He is here," I say strongly, getting angry now. I ignore his request and try to back out of his grip.

Sighing, he lets me go enough to gently grab my hand, and then he starts pulling me into another living room. This one has three desks and two sofas, so I'm guessing an office. The asshole that's dragged me here shouts to a familiar-looking, dark-haired man making out with a pretty blonde, who's grinding on his lap.

"Seb, come here a sec." I frown at him as he winks at me.

Asshole, I have decided his name is Asshole, pulls me in front of him by grabbing my hips gently, but it's clear I can't move if I wanted to. *I kind of don't want to.* What is wrong with me? This man is a stranger, and I'm in my brothers' house and meant to be worrying about meeting them all for the first time.

The guy, Seb, kisses the girl gently then whispers something. She giggles and moves off of him. She slowly glares at me, looking me up and down before moving out of the room. I look back to see this 'Seb' now in front of me, and he is scowling as he looks me over.

Seb? Maybe that's short for Sebastian. I remember that's one of my brothers' names. I look at him closely; I can see it the minute I look at his eyes. *Just like mine.* Sebastian looks nearly as tall as Harley but slightly shorter, I think. His hair's cut short and looks perfect, done in a messy 'I just got out of bed' way. Sebastian is just as muscular as Harley, like he said they all are. My brothers must all go to the gym Harley owns, but as I look further, I see can Sebastian has a black eye and a cut lip. The asshole behind me is just as muscular, making me wonder if he goes to the gym a lot, too. *I wonder if I can go just to see him take his top off.*

"Who's this?" he asks Asshole behind me, maybe Hot-as-fuck Asshole is more appropriate for a nick-name. Sebastian looks down at me with mild curiosity. "I've not seen you before, and I know everyone who's invited here. You are not," he says in a matter of fact way, and its pisses me off a little. But, with one smell, I know he has had a lot of alcohol tonight. So,

I'm going to guess he might be nicer when he isn't drunk.

"She won't tell me her name, just that she is waiting for Harley. Which is crazy, but she is beautiful, so I think we should let her stay," Asshole says from behind me, like I'm not right in front of him.

At that moment, the music stops, and the house is suddenly silent and dark. The guys ignore me as they talk about the electricity going off and who is going to fix it. A few minutes later, as Sebastian tells some guy to go to check the electric, Harley stomps into the room. When he meets my eyes, I see pure anger in them, which is directed at the guy holding me. Before I know it, the Asshole is on the floor, while I'm pushed behind my brother's back.

"Blake! What the fuck? Don't touch her again," he growls at the asshole on the floor, who looks shocked. He turns to me, asking gently, "You did tell him that you were waiting for me, right?"

I nod, smirking a little, and reply, "Yes, but the asshole wouldn't listen."

Harley laughs lightly then turns back to Asshole, aka Blake, and Sebastian, who is still frowning at me. Harley exhales before looking at his brother.

Before he gets a chance to say anything, Sebastian loudly asks, "Who's this? Is this your new girlfriend? I think she looks a bit young for you, man." He laughs.

"No, fuck no, she isn't my girlfriend. I'll explain it all to you when all of us are here and the house is empty. So, start chucking them out." He huffs and sits on the sofa. I wait for a little, until he frowns at me and gestures for me to sit by him.

"Tell me now, who is she?" Sebastian asks rudely, moving to stand in front of the sofa and looking down at me like he's trying to work out a puzzle.

"Your sister, you idiot. Now get the others, and then we can chat. Her name is Izzy," Harley says with a slight chuckle at Sebastian's face. *Pure shock.*

Sebastian looks shell-shocked for maybe a second, and then he smiles, grabbing me up off the sofa for a hug. I can hardly breathe by the time he drops me, carefully, back onto the sofa and smiles happily before he heads off.

I turn and see Blake standing by the door, inspecting me slowly before smirking, then leaving.

"Who was the asshole?" I ask Harley, trying to act cool.

"Blake. The twins' best friend. I'm sorry, he's just a flirt. You looked like a new girl, and they are always interested in new girls. He won't do anything like that again," Harley says and smiles at me.

Harley's phone starts beeping, and he quickly types some messages to someone on his phone, ignoring me.

I'm kind of happy and sad at that news. Happy, because I'll get to see him again, and sad, because he's my brothers' friend, which I'm guessing makes me off-limits. I remember when Devon and I started dating. Devon is one of Tilly's four brothers. She was mad because she was afraid it would be weird if we broke up, that it would affect our friendship. It was lucky for us that Devon and I broke up a month before her parents made them all move. I don't want to make problems, it's probably best if I stay away from the hot asshole.

I said 'probably,' right?

It takes about an hour before everyone is gone, and Sebastian joins us in the living room, sitting close to me. Sebastian tells us the others are cleaning up and will be down soon. Harley asks if he said anything, and he said he hasn't yet but looks over-excited.

"So, sis, you're blond. Must be from your mother, as you clearly have our outstanding looks and eyes," he grins and ruffles my hair.

I laugh slightly and agree. "She was a little less blond than me, but, yes. I must look more like you guys. She had blue eyes, but I got her height," I say as I look at my two giants of brothers.

At that moment, a tall, black-haired man walks in. He has very similar looks to Sebastian–except he has darker-green eyes and unkempt, wavy, black hair. The man looks just as muscular as my other brothers but with more of a swimmer's build and a smaller waist than Sebastian. The man sits on the sofa next to us, then looks me up and down, frowning.

When he tries to speak, Harley holds his hand up and says, "Wait for Luke, and we will continue this."

I look back at him, running my eyes over his black jeans, black top, and leather jacket. I think he looks like a typical biker dude, whereas Sebastian looks like a rich, prep-school boy in his blue polo shirt and normal jeans.

A second later, a drunken-looking, brown-haired guy stumbles in. The guy sways a little before dropping onto the sofa next to the other guy, who I'm now guessing is Elliot. *So, this must be Luke.*

The twins and I are the same age, meaning his dad must have cheated around the same time he got my mum pregnant. I shudder at that thought, but if Luke is younger, he must have left my mum. *I remind myself to ask for the twins' birthday later.*

He has light-brown hair, which is shaved on each side of his head but thicker on top, and the same green eyes. What really stands out are the tattoos on both of his arms. One looks like a dragon curled around his muscular arm, and the other is more of a Celtic design. Luke mumbles something to Elliot, who just nods before he looks at me super quick with a frown and turns to his brothers, and then Luke talks.

"How come she can stay, but my girls had to leave? That's not fair," he says as he flops back in the seat with a huff.

Harley mutters something about God helping him before answering, "This is Izzy, your sister. Dad's secret daughter. I wasn't sure I had found her, so I didn't say anything until I brought her back to live with us."

There is silence as I glance at each of my brothers. Sebastian grins, pulling me into another side hug. Because he, and the rest of my brothers, are built like rocks, it's hard to breathe again.

"I can't breathe, Sebastian." I stutter, and he drops me quickly.

"Sorry, I forgot you're so small. What are you, like, five feet?" Sebastian laughs.

Before I can answer, Elliot says a little rudely,

"You sure it's her? She has our eyes, and maybe she looks a bit similar, but she is small. She is also blond, and I don't know anyone in our family that is blond," he says, his tone far from nice.

It's true, all the brothers are well over six-feet, and I'm tiny. They all have dark hair, whereas mine is a white-blond colour, and if it wasn't for the eyes, I wouldn't believe it either.

"Yes, I'm certain. I checked her medical records." He glares at Elliot as if challenging him to say anything else, and Elliot looks away with his jaw ticking.

"Right, we have been on the road for hours, and I need to sleep. Izzy, you can sleep in my bed until we order you a new bed tomorrow. My room is the only one clean after the party because I keep it locked." Frowning at my other brothers as he stands up, he ends up shaking his head at their grins.

"Sure, I could do with some sleep. It's nice to meet you all," I reply, standing up and following Harley until a drunken Luke picks me up from behind. Luke turns me around to face him like a doll and hugs me before swinging me around and making me dizzy.

"Welcome to our crazy family, sis," he says and lets me go. Luke stinks of booze and what I think is sex, so I'm damn happy to get away now. I look at Elliot on my way out, and he just turns away. *Well, I couldn't expect everyone to like me.*

I hear Sebastian shout, "Night, sis," as I leave the room, and I follow Harley up the impressive, dark-wooden staircase in the entrance hall.

We end up in a large corridor with many wooden doors, which look like the same wood as the stairs. Harley opens the third door on the left with a key from his pocket, then holds it open for me as he flicks a switch for the lights on the wall. It's a large room, but I don't take in much other than the massive, king-size bed with dark, clean sheets. An enormous window overlooks the trees outside, and a large picture, which looks hand painted, hangs above the bed; it's of a woman overlooking a bar.

"I'll be sleeping in the den, which is in the attic. The stairs are down the corridor to the left, okay?" Harley informs me, and I nod at him as words escape me. Damn, it's not the time to start feeling a little shy now. I have to live with these people.

"Come and get me if you need me." He goes to leave before stopping at the door.

"Oh, I forgot, please borrow one of my tops to sleep in if you want, as your stuff is in the car and the house is a tip until the cleaners come in the morn-ing." He gestures to a walk-in closet.

Harley grabs some clothes and says goodnight before he shuts the door. I walk over and lock it, just to make me feel better, then I grab a top from one of the drawers in the closet and put it on. It's so big it falls to my knees, but it will be fine to sleep in. Leaving my clothes on a chair in the corner of the room, I pull myself into bed. As soon as my head hits the pillow, sleep takes me.

BLAKE

Those eyes, the eyes I've seen on my best friends' countless times, but one look at Izzy, and I was lost. *She is beautiful with her long, blond hair, which looks like silk, and an amazing body to go with it.* I have to admit, I liked her slim waist, nice breasts, and amazing ass. Despite being tiny, her legs looked amazing, and yeah, I've been sitting here drawing her for the last two hours like a dork. *I'm fucking crushing on my best friends' sister.*

Tearing off my last drawing of her, I slip it into my back pocket before cleaning my room a little. Fuck, I haven't been able to stop thinking about her since I saw her last night. I had to have her, but when I found out who she was, I couldn't. Izzy acted like she didn't even like me. I'm hoping it's the innocent vibe she gives out and not that she has some secret boyfriend at her last home.

Izzy must have been nervous yesterday. I had had a little to drink, so I wasn't thinking when I held her close like she belonged to me already. When I first saw her, I thought she was sweet and kind, which went with her looks. But then she opened that beautiful mouth of hers, and she called me an asshole in a room full of men twice the size of her. Yeah, I think that's the moment this need to have her happened. *I might have my work cut out.* I haven't cared about a girl in ages; they are all the same. I will admit I'm not the greatest guy when it comes to girls, but I always tell them it's one night and nothing more. I never lie, and they use me all the same, but maybe I'm not the best person to be thinking of her.

Especially since this girl is my best friends' sister and is off-limits. *So fucking off-limits.* I spent all night thinking of her, and even in her worn clothes, she looked crazy-good.

Grabbing my keys and phone, I hop in my car and drive to the Kings' house. I'd be lying to myself if I said I didn't want to see her, it's my main reason for going. Opening the door like I always have since I first walked in here at thirteen, I feel nervous for the first time. Hell, I even have a key they gave me, and this place has always been a second home. They never lock the damn door, anyway, so a key is pointless. Anyone would have to be mad around here to try to rob the King brothers. I walk into the kitchen to find Elliot talking on his mobile phone.

"Yeah, one hour. All that stuff. Yeah. Fine." He puts the phone down, looking frustrated as he rubs his face.

"Hey, you all right?" he asks, noticing me coming into the room.

"Yeah, just bored. How's the new sister?" I ask, trying to act casual. I need to see her. It's like an itch I need to scratch. At the same time, I know if I have one taste of her, I'll be lost forever. *Which worries the fuck out of me.*

"Out shopping with Sebastian," he laughs, and I do too. Even though Seb is a massive, six-foot man, he still buys everyone's clothes. Seb can shop for hours, and I think Izzy is his new play thing.

"Did you get in much trouble for last night?" I ask. "Harley looked mad," I muse, taking a seat on one of the kitchen stools.

"Not too badly. We just have to work in our spare time at the gym and sort out Izzy's room," he sighs, getting a juice out of the fridge.

"What are you doing today?" I ask in reply. I'm

hoping for a reason I can hang around until she is back. *Yeah, I'm that lame.*

"Izzy's new bed, furniture, and stuff are coming in a bit. We are setting it up for her," he groans.

"I'll help," I say too quickly, and Elliot raises his eyebrows.

"Why? It's boring as shit," he asks in a suspicious voice.

"No plans. I like to help," I say, lying through my teeth. I remember when Elliot's new desk came last month, and I told him 'good luck with that' when he read the instructions and looked to me for help. I try a smile and ignore his knowing stare.

"Okay," he says slowly, eyeing me.

My phone goes off in my pocket, and I'm thankful for the distraction from Elliot's questioning looks at me.

Ivy: Mine tonight. I miss your body ;) xoxo

Dammit, I forgot about her, my 'sort of' girlfriend, not that I asked her out. She just told people. Well, she sleeps with someone new as much as I do, or did, so I didn't correct her. *I should have. When was the last time I saw her?*

I realise it was two weeks ago, and I've got to end this. Even if the girl I can't stop thinking about doesn't want me. I can't act on how much I want her before I sort out my mess.

We need to talk. Meet me at the café in town at 7 p.m.?

Ivy: No, my house. I don't want to talk xoxo

Seriously, at the café or I will say what I have to on this text.

Yeah, that makes me sound like an asshole, but, honestly, I know she doesn't really care about me.

Ivy: Just say it xoxo

Fine. It's over, sorry.

Ivy: What? Why? Was it because I slept with Daniel last weekend? I'll make it up to you ;) xoxo

Daniel is one of my friends, and Elliot and I are going out for drinks with him tonight. I'm surprised he slept with her as he knew I had, and usually we don't do that shit, but it's worse that I really don't give a crap that they did. I really shouldn't have let her think she actually was my girlfriend after I slept with her once, but it was when I was drunk.

No, it's not, but it's over. Don't message me again, I'm sorry.

Fuck, I wrote that without thinking. It's far harsher than I needed to be and she messages back.

Ivy: Asshole

Yeah, I deserve that. I turn my phone off as a van turns up.

"Let's get to work." Luke claps my shoulder as he passes and makes me smile. Five crazy hours later, the room is finally done, and I silently slip my drawing under her pillow and hope she likes it.

Fuck, I'm acting like a girl over her. Not that I can help it. I need to know if she likes me or wants me. I can't remember any girl really, as they were never important. I have a feeling this sexy, innocent girl is the best thing that's ever happened to me. I grin before shaking my head as I walk out of her room.